'Don't you touch me,' Seven warned Jake thickly, a fierce light burning in her grey eyes, giving them the eerie yellow glow of a sky before a storm.

He held up his hands. 'I wouldn't dream of it,' he murmered drily, his brain beginning to function again as the clouds of fury dissipated. He had covered a few boxing matches in his time and he knew the signs of punch-drunkenness when he saw them. Whatever her intentions, little Miss Mouse had evidently taken a pounding.

'You'd better sit down before you fall down,' he told her.

'Go to hell!' She startled herself with her own vehemence.

A snarling mouse. In spite of himself he grinned and watched as she tried to master her weaving limbs.

NO REPRIEVE

BY

SUSAN NAPIER

MILLS & BOON LIMITED
ETON HOUSE   18-24 PARADISE ROAD
RICHMOND   SURREY   TW9 1SR

First published in Great Britain 1990
by Mills & Boon Limited

© Susan Napier 1990

Australian copyright 1990
Philippine copyright 1991
This edition 1991

ISBN 0 263 76917 8

Set in Times Roman 10 on 11 pt.
01-9101-58880 C

Made and printed in Great Britain

Necessity is harsh,
Fate has no reprieve

Euripides

CHAPTER ONE

'MISS SELKIRK?'

Seven's hand tightened involuntarily on the door-handle as she wondered whether to admit to her identity. In this day and age it wasn't wise to be trusting towards strangers who arrived on your doorstep, particularly strangers who looked like this man. Even standing on the step below her he topped her by a good few menacing inches and the expression in his navy eyes was anything but reassuring.

'Well?' he snapped with such arrogant impatience that she found herself automatically nodding, her pale grey eyes wide with apprehension.

'Yes. I'm Miss Selkirk.' Was he a policeman? He certainly had the build for it—under the jeans and black sweater he looked all hard muscle. And there was an air of authority about him that bespoke a man used to getting answers whether they came hard or easily.

'May I come in?' It wasn't a request, it was a demand, and she had to struggle against the impulse to instinctively obey. She mustn't let his rudeness intimidate her into doing anything foolish.

'Have you got any identification?' she asked cautiously.

'My name should be identification enough,' he told her grimly. 'Jake Jackson.'

It was more than enough. Recognition shot her through with instant horror. Visions of lurid headlines danced before her eyes. She jumped back, slamming the door, but his reactions had been honed by years of foot-in-the-door experience and he was there before her. He swore as the heavy wood crushed his silver-tipped boot, but he didn't withdraw. Instead he twisted, bunting the door with shoulder and hip, sending Seven staggering back into the hall as he stepped inside and kicked the door shut behind him.

'Thank you,' he said smoothly, as if she had acted the gracious hostess instead of trying to shut him out like a rabid dog.

'You can't come in here,' she protested breathlessly, her heart pounding with fear.

'Why not? With a *client*, are you?' The sneer, sounding vaguely obscene, bewildered her.

'I—— You have no right——'

'No?' He was looking around the shabby hall, lit only by the late afternoon sun which streamed in through the stained glass windows on either side of the front entranceway, throwing a patchwork of rich colours on the polished wood floor. His eyes fell on the door to what Aunt Jane liked to call the 'front parlour', and Seven stiffened. Her movement was barely perceptible and he wasn't even facing her but he must have sensed something in the air for he shot her a grimly triumphant snarl of a smile over his shoulder as he headed for the door.

'No! You can't go in there!' she panicked. She knew she couldn't stop him by physical force, her five feet three would be ludicrously ineffective against his six-foot-plus frame, so she tried a reckless threat. 'If you don't leave immediately, I'm calling the police!'

He stopped and turned, hands on his hips. 'Are you, now?' he said softly, and she mistook the softness for uncertainty. She nodded too vigorously in her relief.

'You're trespassing,' she pointed out bravely.

He shrugged. 'So? Call.' Adding with deceptive casualness, 'But make it the Fraud Squad. They'll be more than interested in my reason for being here.'

'Fraud Squad?' Seven's courage wavered. Wherever Jake Jackson went scandal inevitably followed—scandal, and the full glare of the public spotlight. He was a muck-raker, pure and simple, and someone as vulnerable as Seven would make an easy target for his infamous brand of mud-slinging.

'I suppose you figured that I'd be afraid of the pub-licity,' he ground at her. 'But you chose the wrong victim. I specialise in exposing people like you, and this time it's going to be my very personal pleasure to feed someone through the meat grinder. It's about time the *Clarion* launched another crusade.'

Seven's heart lurched. His newspaper's crusades were a New Zealand media legend, crudely and often cruelly effective. 'I'm afraid I don't know what you're talking about,' she said feebly, earning herself another look of raking contempt from the dark eyes.

'Your ghoulish scam,' he informed her tersely. 'How many other people have you bled of their hopes and their money? How many times have you fed the deepest fears and misguided superstitions of gullible victims in order to make a fast buck?'

'That sounds more like a description of your editorial policy than of me,' she snapped with uncharacteristic rashness. She quickly regretted it as his eyes narrowed dangerously.

'You're denying it?' he demanded savagely.

She made a fluttering gesture of puzzlement with her hands. 'Denying what? I truly don't know what you're talking about.' At least she hoped she didn't. Balancing the conflicting demands of past guilt and present duty with her desire for a life of quiet privacy had been no easy task, but she had thought that she had managed it rather well. Had someone betrayed her? But who? And why? She helped, not harmed.

'No?' He spun with easy strength and thrust open the door behind him to reveal the parlour in all its overblown glory: the bead curtains that divided the room in two, the exotic floor rugs with their mythical and zodiacal signs, the dark flocked oriental wallpaper and, most damning of all, the black-velvet-covered round table on which sat a highly polished crystal ball.

Seven could feel herself flushing and poked nervously at the thick coil of brown hair at the nape of her neck, wishing she had a fringe to hide behind as his sweeping survey condemned both the room and her. She was resigned to living with Aunt Jane's increasingly eccentric taste and thought she had long got over the compulsive need to apologise for it. She wasn't going to be bullied into it now, either, but knew that she had to say something in the face of his silent sneer.

'I——' The trouble was, what *could* she say in defence of a décor that screamed its lack of style and taste?

'Let me guess,' he interrupted her with heavy sarcasm. 'You sublet to gypsies.'

Her flush deepened. 'Of course not, this is…this is…'

'Where Madame Zoe cons the suckers out of their money with a collection of cheap theatrical tricks?' He moved into the florid room and after a stunned instant Seven followed.

'She does not!' She was mystified by the man's ill-concealed rage. Charging a friend a few dollars to read tea leaves or palms or gaze into a crystal ball was hardly the earth-shatteringly evil fraud that he was implying.

'Oh, come, *Madame*, there's no need to hide behind coy pronouns——'

'Me?' Seven's mouth dropped open. She was suddenly overcome with a vast rush of relief as she realised what had happened. 'You think *I'm* Madame Zoe? But I'm not!'

'No?' Again that simple little negative that expressed a world of scepticism. 'You've admitted you're Jane Selkirk——'

'No! No, I'm not. Jane is my *aunt*. We live together.' He appeared unconvinced. 'I'm her niece,' she added redundantly.

For the first time his dark blue eyes focused on her rather than past her and Seven had to brace herself to accept the intensive stare without blushing guiltily. Her toes curled in her sensible black shoes, but her hands remained determinedly relaxed at her sides and her small face was held carefully blank. She knew she looked the picture of what she was, a reassuringly normal human being—as far from exotic as it was possible to be. She wore just enough make-up to add a little necessary colour to her cool, quiet eyes but not enough to emphasise them. The hair drawn tidily off her face revealed a pale, delicate forehead and neat features. In fact, everything about her was neat and tidy, from her small nose and prim upper lip to the plain white cotton blouse and dark tailored skirt that she had worn to work. The only thing that hinted at any contradiction to the overall impression of genteel respectability was the generous fullness of her lower lip, a provocative curve which she had an unconscious tendency to hide by nibbling.

While he was studying her Seven had no choice but to stare back. Now she was no longer governed by her initial fright she realised that Jake Jackson was a very good-looking man, if you liked hard-bitten, cynical men, which Seven didn't. He certainly didn't look like the kind of bloated, slavering moral cripple that she had pictured as owner-editor of a newspaper that specialised in plumbing the depths of human depravity. His clothes, though casual, were expensive, and he wore them with both ease and style. His dark brown hair was thick and slightly longer than collar-length, shaped to his head but still managing to look like a noticeable statement of individuality in a man long past the juvenile years of defiance against traditional standards. Late thirties and

every year showing, thought Seven meanly, in an attempt
to downplay the attractions of that lived-in face. Some
women—a lot of women—would find the lines of experience combined with the masculine symmetry of those
high cheekbones, the hawkish nose and that bold jaw
exciting. Seven found it intimidating. She preferred men
who were sure enough of their masculinity to be gentle,
sensitive... This man looked as if he would be as sensitive as an armadillo!

His continuing silence was beginning to make her
nervous. It was on the tip of her tongue to demand
sarcastically whether he had seen enough, but she had
the feeling that instead of putting him in his place her
sarcasm might backfire. What if he said no? She would
blush, she knew she would, and stammer like an idiot
and amuse him with her ridiculous naïveté. Seven was
no good at banter. In her imagination she was sophis-
ticated and assured and the most acid of wits, but in
real life she was too aware of other people to possess the
freedom of true unselfconsciousness.

She cleared her throat. 'Er...my aunt isn't here at the
moment.' It had suddenly occurred to her what she had
done. In her anxiety to escape this man's wrath she had
thrust Aunt Jane squarely into his path. 'I don't know
what time she'll be home,' she lied hurriedly, pleased
that her habit of tidiness had led her to throw away the
note which her aunt had left under the magnet on the
door of the fridge. She wouldn't put it past Jake Jackson
to search the premises! 'Perhaps you could come back
later,' she added hopefully, with a nervous twitch she
hoped would pass for an innocent smile.

It didn't.

'Where is she?'

'I'm not sure,' Seven said vaguely. His stare didn't
waver and she could feel the guilty blush sweep up from
the soles of her feet. Any moment it was going to crest
the neck of her blouse and reveal itself. 'L-look, why

don't you tell me what this is about?' she said earnestly, to take her mind off the incipient blush. 'I'm sure it's just a simple misunderstanding. My aunt has never done anything illegal in her life. She's a harmless old lady——'

'Harmless!' That cracked his stony façade. 'I don't call extortion harmless!'

'Extortion!' Guilt and embarrassment vanished like smoke in the face of such absurdity. 'Now I *know* this is all a mistake. I don't know where you got your evidence from, but you've definitely got the wrong person.'

'Do you know of another Jane Selkirk alias Madame Zoe who advertises herself in the personal column——?'

'Of your paper?' Seven scoffed. 'Aunt Jane would never *read* your paper, let alone advertise in it!'

Something glinted in his navy eyes. 'No, not the *Clarion*. Even we draw the line at out-and-out charlatans. Massage parlours and escort agencies are our limit.' This damning admission was made without the slightest hint of apology, but before Seven could express her outrage at his comparing Aunt Jane unfavourably to such sleaze he was continuing harshly, 'You can cut out all the wide-eyed innocence, Miss Selkirk. I don't buy it. You know damned well what this room is decked out for!'

'If you're talking about Aunt Jane's fortune-telling, of course I know about it, but there's nothing illegal about being interested in spiritualism. It's just an old woman's hobby. My aunt is in her mid-sixties and she's getting a bit eccentric in her old age, but that's not a crime. You must be scraping the bottom of the barrel for stories if you have to come around harassing old-age pensioners——'

'I don't call it a hobby when your aunt is offering her professional services in exchange for money——'

'A few dollars, and I'd hardly call it a professional service. It's just a bit of fun between friends. Nobody takes it seriously!' Seven protested, her heart beginning to flutter uncomfortably, the way it always did when she was forced into a stressful confrontation.

'You're very privileged, if you can dismiss thousands of dollars so lightly. I wonder whether the IRS might be interested in a "hobby" that generates so much income. Has your aunt filed a tax return in the last few years——?'

By now Seven was thoroughly upset. It was like talking to a brick wall, and a thick one at that! Nothing made the slightest impact. All her instincts were prompting her to run away from the unequal battle, but for Aunt Jane's sake she had to try. She took a deep breath to calm herself.

'Mr Jackson, we seem to be talking at cross purposes. Perhaps if you'd calm down and tell me exactly what my aunt is supposed to have done we can clear this up without it going any further.' She spoke with the slow, quiet firmness that always seemed to work in the hushed environs of the library. Unfortunately the voice of sweet reason sounded, in the circumstances, like the hint of a bribe.

'Without the police being involved, you mean,' he said grimly. 'Forget it. That might have worked for you in the past, but you're not buying your aunt out of this one.'

'I wasn't offering to. I was just proposing saving *you* the embarrassment of a public apology,' Seven said tightly. 'If you print any lies about my aunt, we'll sue.'

'I'll look forward to it,' he sneered and to her dismay she realised he meant it. Being the unprincipled man he was, he would relish any opportunity for public exposure.

Either way Aunt Jane would suffer and, by association, Seven, too.

'Why?' she asked in hurt bewilderment. 'Why are you doing this? What have we ever done to you?' For she had suddenly realised that there must be more involved here than mere professional interest in getting a story. His anger was too personal, too intense. She tried to remember everything he had said since he had smashed his way into the house, but he wasn't giving her time to reorder her thoughts.

'You can ask that?'

'Will you stop answering every question with another question?' she cried in frustration. 'Can't you give me a straight answer for a change?'

His eyes narrowed. 'You mean you really don't know?'

She took a sharp, hissing breath, which was as dramatic a display of emotion as she allowed herself. Her hands clenched at her side to quell the unaccustomed desire to hit him. Seven hated violence, physical or emotional. 'No, I don't know,' she said with rigid patience, through her teeth.

'My mother was sent a copy of Madame Zoe's advertisement through the mail——'

'Just a minute—what advertisement?' interrupted Seven quickly. She wanted there to be no more misunderstandings.

He made an impatient sound under his breath, but, after giving her a darkly suspicious look under gathered brows, he dug around in the back pocket of his jeans. He flipped open a snakeskin wallet, giving Seven a brief glimpse of a colour photograph tucked into one of the transparent plastic credit card holders. Was it a woman? His wife? Girlfriend? No, make that lover, she thought wryly. Jake Jackson looked too intensely masculine to be satisfied with a relationship of platonic innocence. He would want it all...and so, no doubt, would his woman.

Seven shifted uneasily at her thoughts. Her own deeply private nature made the idea of invading the privacy of others anathema. She only did so when it was unavoidable. She avoided it now by hastily taking the neatly folded cutting that Jake Jackson had extracted from his wallet and concentrating on that instead. She read the small, boxed advertisement with a growing distress.

'Lost a Loved One?' asked the bold typeface. 'Do not despair. Contact is always possible on the Astral Plane. Death and disappearance are merely physical demanifestations. In the spiritual world all is knowledge. Know your future, discover your past, find what has been lost. Madame Zoe can help you. Appointment absolutely necessary.' And there, at the end, in black and white, was the suburban address and phone number of the house where they stood.

Seven closed her eyes, a bitter taste in her mouth at the betrayal.

Oh, Aunt Jane, why have you done this to me?

'Well?'

She opened her eyes reluctantly. 'I had no idea that she had put this in the paper.'

He didn't comment, but his suspicion was like a weight pressing against her innocence.

'You—you said she received it through the mail?' She didn't really want to know, but she had to ask, 'Do you know who sent it?'

'In the circumstances, do you need to ask?' he enquired harshly. 'There was a note with it which offered information to which nobody else had access.'

'Information? About what?'

His suspicion was instantly intensified as he bit back a dark epithet. 'Don't try and play games with me, Miss Selkirk, I'm not in the mood. I might be prepared to consider the possibility that you could be ignorant about the extortion, but that's as far as my credulity stretches. Anyone who was truly innocent would have made the connection.'

'What connection?' Seven whispered, genuinely bewildered.

'With my missing daughter!' he exploded. 'My God, you're not going to pretend that you didn't know about *that*! It was plastered all over the Press and television for months at the time, and even featured on a *CrimeStop* programme recently, which is when I presume your aunt had her bright idea to milk my mother.'

'I don't watch television,' said Seven unevenly.

'You do *read* though, I presume?' he said with heavy sarcasm.

'Books. I hardly look at the local newspapers.' That was a lie. She actively avoided looking at them. She kept abreast of current events by reading the serious journals and overseas newspapers that arrived in the library, in the sure knowledge that the relentless tales of human tragedy encapsulated in their pages had been safely filtered by time and distance.

He looked justifiably incredulous. After all, Jake Jackson had become rich and famous off the modern fetish for being bombarded with needless information at all hours of the night and day.

'I told you no games, dammit!' he swore viciously. 'You'll not find me the easy mark my mother is. I can play a hell of a lot rougher than you, especially when my family is at stake.' He looked truly murderous as he prowled menacingly closer, and for the first time Seven felt the presence of the black pain which was fuelling his white-hot fury. She instinctively stepped back, both mentally and physically, crushing her stirring compassion.

'I'm not lying,' she told him quietly. 'I had no idea that your daughter was missing. I don't even listen to the radio much. I prefer to play records and tapes.'

Instead of dousing his anger her explanation seemed to goad him further. 'How in the hell can you function if you don't know what the rest of humanity is doing?

Don't you care? Doesn't it matter to you? What do you do—spend all day with your head in the sand?'

She squared her slender shoulders under the crisp blouse. 'I'm a city council librarian.'

'A librarian!' His eyes flicked back over the clichéd primness of her attire. 'You certainly dress the part, but you don't act it very well. I thought you people were supposed to be well informed! I thought libraries were supposed to be the storehouses of our popular culture. My God, how many more of you are there out there... people we never reached, people who pride themselves on their damned intellectual isolation?'

He swung away from her and slammed his fist into the wall, and she knew that he wished the wall were her. He had obviously put great store on nationwide publicity to help him get his daughter back, and now he was face to face with the flaw in his plan.

'I'm sorry,' she said helplessly.

He rounded on her. 'Sorry! Oh, yes, you will be. Because this is one piece of nasty news that you *won't* be able to avoid any longer. When my mother, in her desperation, kept an appointment with Madame Zoe she was asked for money, a great deal of money, in exchange for information about Rebecca.'

Seven's pale skin went almost transparent with shock.

'I don't believe it. My aunt would never do anything so cruel. Your mother must have misunderstood... If my aunt intended to ask for money, why didn't she approach you, or your wife——?'

He seemed to relish her shock as a small down payment on revenge. 'I haven't got a wife. Your aunt no doubt chose my mother because she discovered that she was a vulnerable old woman, made pathetically gullible by tragedy. *You* may wear blinkers, but your aunt obviously doesn't. My mother is publicly on record as saying that she would do *anything*, *pay* anything, to get her precious only grandchild back.'

'Wouldn't *you*?' Seven asked, desperate not to believe her aunt's eccentricity could have slid into such decline.

The navy-blue eyes were suddenly black with raging violence. 'Oh, I'll find out what happened to Rebecca, if it takes the rest of my life and everything I have. And whoever took her from me is going to spend the rest of *their* life regretting it. But that doesn't mean I'm willing to grovel at the feet of every crank and low-life that crawls out of the woodwork, and, believe me, there were a hundred of them—sick, twisted, greedy people who only muddied the waters and obscured the *real* clues. And now your crazy aunt wants to dredge the cesspit and stir up my mother's anguish all over again just as she was beginning to accept——'

Seven moistened her lips. 'If...if Aunt Jane approached your mother I'm sure it was out of a genuine belief that she could help——' She tried to conquer her deepening unease, no longer completely convinced of her ground. He was so *sure* of his facts that his certainty vanquished hers. 'I...she's a...a respected ...psychic——'

'The phrase is a contradiction in terms,' he ridiculed contemptuously. 'If your aunt had any genuine information she could have laid it with the proper authorities—the police. There's still a fifty-thousand-dollar reward on offer, but your aunt knew damned well her mumbo jumbo wouldn't qualify for it, so she decided to try to approach my mother personally. You can imagine the shock she caused, to a woman who's not in the best of health. Unfortunately for "Madame Zoe" my mother may be gullible but she can't keep a secret to save her life, she's too honest, to open herself to understand duplicity in others. Thank God it's not an inherited trait!'

While he was speaking Seven had sat down with a thump in the big, uncomfortably overstuffed chair that

Madame Zoe's 'visitors' were directed to, her legs no longer capable of supporting her.

'W…what sort of information was my aunt offering?'

'No more protestations of an innocent misunderstanding?' he sneered.

Seven's hands twisted tightly in her lap as she ignored the unimportant question of her aunt's guilt. 'What did she tell your mother?'

He shrugged in disgust. 'Precious little. The first session was obviously just the teaser to lead up to the demand for money. She mentioned a few personal details about my daughter, things that anyone might have picked up from the papers. She assured my mother that she "knew" from the "auras" surrounding her photographs that Rebecca was still safe—a fact that even the police have acknowledged unlikely in the extreme——' it was said flatly, without inflexion, and Seven looked away from his shuttered face, not wanting to see what he didn't want seen '—but that she was "troubled". The inference my mother naturally drew, the one your aunt *wanted* her to draw, was that if she left any stone, no matter how bizarre, unturned she might be condemning her own granddaughter to some living hell or horrifying death——'

'No!' Seven's cry was bloodless, weak. A protest against the sympathy that was bleeding through her. 'How…how old is your daughter? How long has she been missing?' No wonder he looked haggard and hard-edged.

She had expected him to reply a few months, so she was shocked to the core when he said baldly, 'She would have been eight this week. She'd just had her second birthday when she disappeared.'

'Six *years*?' Oh, God, no! *No!* A silent scream filled her head. Her grey eyes clouded with horror.

'Yes. Six years. A long time. Too long for me to have any tolerance left for some callous crone who turns up out of the blue to rip apart my mother's peace of mind all over again.'

'Blonde and blue eyes, and a chased-gold locket around her neck,' whispered Seven numbly.

His big body tensed, his face chiselled rigid by anger mixed with a savage suspicion. 'So you *do* know about her.' He pounced on the discrepancy. 'Just what exactly do you know? Do you have some information about my daughter...about your aunt? Dammit, don't just stand there like a pillar of salt, *tell* me!' He caught her fragile forearm and hauled her to her feet, shaking her out of her numbed silence.

'You're hurting me!'

'I haven't even begun. *Tell me what you know!*'

'I don't know anything! I just remember seeing her picture in the paper, that's all.' And since then had done her best to forget... This was her punishment!

He didn't believe her, her reaction had been too extreme. 'You don't read the papers, remember? And after all this time you instantly knew what she looked like? You're lying——'

'No! I...I saw a photograph of ...I saw a photograph of her recently, that's all,' she stammered, trying to turn aside his frightening rage. 'Aunt Jane is a great hoarder...she hardly ever throws things away. The back room is filled with years old junk that she insists that she might need one day. I got some old newspapers from there last week—to wrap the rubbish in. I just happened to notice the picture on the front page.' But she couldn't tell him why. She had told her aunt, though, to her evident cost!

'And?'

'And nothing!'

He let her go, violently, so that the release was a punishment in itself. She massaged the blood back into her arm, welcoming the pain as a distraction from her growing guilt.

'I'm sorry about your little girl,' she managed to whisper at last. 'And I'm sorry for any anguish that my aunt might have caused——'

'*Might?*'

'All right, *has* caused. But I'm sure that in her own mind she only wanted to help. That's all she ever wants to do. The money—well—that was wrong, but maybe she just got carried away with her own importance. She's getting old and she can be . . . very vague——'

'You mean, senile,' he said cruelly.

She swallowed. Nothing had been resolved, but she didn't want to be drawn into another long argument. She felt sick and cold and just wanted to be left alone with her guilt.

'I think it's time you went, Mr Jackson. I'll tell my aunt that you called . . .' She trailed off, despising herself for her feebleness and knowing that he did, too, as he gave her a look of dismissive contempt.

'Do that. Tell her to call me if she's willing to be interviewed. I wouldn't want to print a story that was *entirely* one-sided!' He thrust a business card into her cold, nerveless fingers.

She didn't have the energy to resent his sarcasm. 'I . . . you'll have to talk to my aunt,' was Seven's blind reply as she brushed past him, out of the claustrophobic closeness of the parlour.

'Believe me, I will. If she doesn't contact me, I'll assume that she'd rather talk to the police. He followed her stiffened back along the hallway and waited as she fumbled nervously with the front door.

'Goodbye, Mr Jackson.' She would have liked to push him out of the door with all speed, but she didn't dare touch him, shrinking at the idea of personal contact. She could feel the waves of pain building inside her skull. If he chose to dig his heels in and refuse to be hustled away she was going to be physically ill. She refused to look at him as he lingered, but she could feel his hot eyes burning through her paper-thin composure and knew that her disturbed behaviour was only confirming his suspicions. But she no longer cared *what* he thought, as long as he was gone.

When his footsteps had finally died away she retreated shakily to the reassuringly plain and functional kitchen. She made herself a strong, hot cup of coffee and for good measure poured in a slug of Aunt Jane's 'medicinal' whisky. It tasted awful but it stopped the shaking.

What was she going to do? How was she going to stop that awful man from carrying out his threats? She cupped her hands around the painfully hot mug. If Aunt Jane had demanded money for what, in the past, she had always performed for free or the merest token amount, then that awful man had every right to feel the way he did and to take steps to make sure that it didn't happen again. However much she might despise his particular style of journalism, she couldn't doubt that he had loved his daughter and that his own helplessness at the time of her disappearance had enraged him. That was probably partly why he had come storming over here... because it was something active he *could* do in defence of his family. How well Seven knew the utter frustration of helplessness, of being at the mercy of others, but, whereas she had coped by withdrawing and controlling, Jake Jackson responded to the whims of blind fate with physical action, lashing out at everything in his path.

If only she didn't understand so well, thought Seven in despair. That was her curse—to understand. It always undermined her ability to sustain an argument, because she could see so clearly the validity of her opponent's viewpoint, however personal or ill-advised. To understand was to forgive and that made her incapable of selfishness or malice. The trouble was that everyone needed an element of selfishness in their nature, just to survive. People thought that because she was quiet and shy to the point of timidity she was weak. Only Seven knew that such weakness had been her salvation.

Out in his car Jake Jackson sat for long minutes trying to bring himself under control. His hands were actually shaking and his knuckles whitened as he gripped the steering-wheel to control the weakness. He ached with the need for violent action but there would have been little point in taking out his frustration on that frightened wisp of a woman in the house. She had felt so fragile between his hands that he could have snapped her in two with a twitch of his wrists. He doubted that she was as innocent as she pretended, but on the other hand he couldn't believe that anyone so feeble could knowingly have assisted a crime. Too timid...too transparently obvious. She hadn't even been able to withstand the lightest pressure without folding like a piece of paper. If she had had any real guilty knowledge it would have come stammering nervously out. She had probably just got rattled trying to figure out how to protect her aunt from the appalling consequences of her actions. Certainly she had seemed genuinely shocked by the idea of blackmail.

His death-grip on the wheel loosened and his mouth cracked a grim smile as he remembered that sedate horror, the big, vague eyes, the mousy hair in its fussy bun, and the equally mousy whisper that she had sunk to when he had frightened her. Yes...sedate...the word suited her. She was probably the archetypal spinster librarian—a tyrannical horror at work to overcompensate for her mousiness everywhere else. She didn't look as if she had an ounce of gumption in her whole scrawny body, her bit of bravado about calling the police vanishing like spit on a hot plate at the merest hint of scandal.

Yes...the niece might definitely be useful if the aunt proved a tough nut to crack—and crack her he would.

Someone had to pay. Accepting that Rebecca had gone forever had been a long, hard road to travel, but he had made it in the end, without crippling his sanity with self-destructive guilt and regrets. And his mother would, too, with the right kind of help. She must be made to see that it wasn't a matter of faith, or lack of it, any more, it was a matter of survival. And any outsider who threatened that survival was signing a warrant for their own destruction.

CHAPTER TWO

'How dare you do such a thing?'

'But, Seven, dear, all I did was offer to help.' Jane Selkirk's bewildered protest was sincere. 'That *poor* woman ... Do you know what it's been like for her, over the years? Everyone else has given up, even the police and the child's own father. Why, Charlotte Jackson was so grateful to hear something positive that she was practically falling over herself to offer me a reward!'

Seven bit her lower lip to stop the flood of unkind words bursting through the dam of her much-tried patience.

'That's not quite the point, Aunt Jane. It's a question of morality. Mr Jackson said that the money wasn't offered, it was *demanded*——'

'Mr Jackson is a sceptic.' Jane Selkirk pronounced the sentence with disdain, as if it explained everything.

Seven sighed in exasperation.

It was at times like this she felt as if she were the guardian, rather than the other way around, but she couldn't find it in her heart to resent the burden. When Aunt Jane had taken in the twelve-year-old Seven and her twin sister Morgan after their parents had died she had done it in the full knowledge of the hardship involved. Apart from the fact that she was a middle-aged spinster with no experience of children, there had been no money to provide for their upbringing. Her brother Carl had been a generous, improvident man, always ready to pour what money he did manage to save into the pockets of those more needy, or into some new and spectacular scheme to improve the circus which was his life. Tomorrow never bothered Carl, he and the tiny, light-hearted acrobat that he had met and married in the space of a week enjoyed each day that came with all the considerable optimism of their warm natures. The circus had its ups and downs but Carl and Fay Selkirk had lived charmed lives until that stark winter night a fire had raged through the caravan that was their home. There was little to be salvaged from the ashes. The twins had come to live in the alien surroundings of suburbia with nothing but the clothes they'd stood up in, and Seven would be ever grateful for the way that Jane Selkirk had accepted them with open arms, and never once showed the bewilderment or resentment that she must at times have felt over the disruption to her comfortable lifestyle by a pair of difficult youngsters.

Seven and Morgan had been used to a gypsy existence that was an uneven mixture of hard work and responsibility and wild freedom. It hadn't been easy to adjust to the rigid rules of polite behaviour demanded by their new surroundings, or to get used to living in one place for more than a few weeks at a time and attend a regular school which had a whole new set of different rules to abide by. Each girl had done it in her own way. Whereas Morgan, as soon as she was old enough, had left to continue the peripatetic life that she had known as a child, Seven had grown to love her new-found peace and security and had been quite content to stay on as loving companion to her aunt as the years took their toll. At twenty-six she felt that she was at last coming to agreeable terms with herself...until something like this happened.

Looking at her aunt, Seven was aware of the acute irony of the situation. As she herself had become more conservative, Jane Selkirk had become correspondingly more 'free-spirited' until now their positions were almost totally reversed. She hoped that her own tolerance would prove as enduring as her aunt's had formerly been. The trouble was that, whatever else Aunt Jane had lost, she had retained her immutable conviction that she knew best. Arguments to the contrary were usually a fruitless waste of energy.

Seven frowned broodingly as she watched her aunt stir a pot that didn't need stirring. Her aunt was about her own height, but there any resemblance ceased. Where Seven was fine-boned like her mother, Jane took after the Selkirk side of the family and was roundly built. With her twinkling brown eyes and soft wrinkles and sprightly gait she would have been the epitome of a sweet little old lady if it hadn't been for the awesome and totally false blackness of her hair and the bizarre clothes that she had taken to collecting. Seven had watched, disquieted by the gradual metamorphosis from ageing gentility to full-blown eccentricity. But what right had she to dictate that Aunt Jane shouldn't enjoy a colourful twilight in what had been a largely colourless life?

'Aunt Jane?' The sudden bite in her voice surprised them both. 'We had an agreement, remember? You promised that you would be *discreet*——'

'But I was. I approached Mrs Jackson very quietly. She's a rich woman, Seven. She's used to paying for quality. She wouldn't have taken me seriously if I hadn't put everything on a businesslike footing. It was partly *because* I asked for a worthwhile sum that she believed that I could do it——'

'That you could do what?' asked Seven with suddenly ominous quietness. 'What did you tell her you could do?'

It was even worse than she had feared. This time Madame Zoe hadn't contented herself with vague promises, she had over-reached herself with epic skill. She had boasted to Charlotte Jackson that she could succeed where the police had failed, and had produced her bulging scrap-book of clippings about successful 'cases' and letters of thanks to prove it. She had stopped short of offering a money-back guarantee, but not short enough. She had virtually promised results. The only saving grace in the whole rotten affair was that she hadn't insisted on the money as cash up-front.

'How could you be so cruel as to raise someone's hopes like that?' Seven raged with unaccustomed temper. 'The only excuse I can think of for you is that you might have got confused by your own publicity. Well, that's it. No more. It's got to stop. You're no more psychic than...than Jake Jackson is!'

Jane Selkirk seemed to shrink before her niece's quiet anger, but she refused to give up.

'No, but *you* are. And you were very sure that Rebecca Jackson was alive, you said so. You thought that meant that she must have been found, but I went into the central library last week and looked up the files and found out that she hadn't. I thought her family would like to know, too——'

'Know what? I don't actually *know* anything,' Seven pointed out wearily, 'and I told you, the feeling was too vague to pin down.'

'Because you didn't want to. But you could find out. If you really wanted to you could find out.'

'No!' Seven recoiled from the thought. 'For goodness' sake, Aunt Jane, it's been years...too many years. What I felt could have just been an echo of her existence...'

'She was kidnapped, Seven. Stolen from the heart of her family. It's *you* who's being cruel, not me. You're abandoning that little girl all over again.'

Seven was hunched on the kitchen chair, pressing the delicate bones of her face with her slender hands, trying to stop the darkness from flooding her brain. But it was no use. Never had she resented her unwelcome gift more bitterly. For years she had resisted its intrusion into her life, had tried to shrug off those chills of certain knowledge that could suddenly sweep out of nowhere and overwhelm her with bizarre thoughts and images. Only when they had become too intrusive had she allowed herself to open herself up to them. It had been

like harbouring another being within, someone over
whom she had no control and who at times managed to
control *her*. Only Morgan had truly understood the way
she felt, and even that closeness was compromised by
the fact that her twin had grown up to accept the power
they both possessed as something entirely natural, to be
utilised freely. Morgan had never had any qualms about
their circus act. She had never shared Seven's childish
frustration at knowing that while the audiences had
wildly applauded the twins' mind-reading and magic act
with their father none of them had ever really believed
that any of it was real. The supreme irony was that the
crowds had always preferred the flashy trickery that their
father had fleshed out the act with to the dramatic
moments of genuine extra-sensory perception. They
preferred to baffle over what trick Morgan had used to
discover that the man in the second row had a knotted
piece of string in his pocket than to hear of some im-
pending accident or bereavement. One went to the circus
to be thrilled and awed—to laugh not to cry—and it was
a bitter fact that most of the twins' perceptions involved
the darker side of life. Fear, grief, and rage seemed to
emit stronger vibrations than love or happiness.

So it had been with Rebecca Jackson. Seven had been
peeling potatoes into a sheet of newspaper that had been
wrapped around some knick-knack of Aunt Jane's
recently rescued from the back room when the headline
'Toddler Still Missing' had caught her attention. Her eyes
had automatically flown to the dateline and she had
relaxed when she realised that it was more than five years
old. Safe.

She had brushed the peelings away and studied the
photograph of the missing child. The round, dimpled
face was alight with some unexplained joy, the fluffy
blonde curls as bouncy as her big smile, the eyes that
the description below said were blue were large and
sweetly innocent. Seven had felt the warm surge of energy

that she always associated with a strong life-force flow over her and had been further relieved. Whatever had happened to the little girl, it had not been death. There was a vague undercurrent of unease associated with that lively warmth, but nothing like the sharp, jagged warnings that had always presaged a tragedy.

The unease had not disappeared when she had skimmed fitfully through the story, subconsciously blanking out the child's name, denying her the reality of an identity, and selecting only what she herself wanted to know. The two-year-old had been abducted from a shopping centre a month previous to the newspaper's date. The whole tenor of the story suggested a scaling down of an unsuccessful enquiry. A quote from the police inspector in charge of the investigation mentioned the fact that there had been only one unconfirmed sighting of a man with the child in his car, and no ransom demand had ever been received. His statement that the police now 'had grave fears for the child's safety' had given Seven a nasty shock, but she'd dismissed the idea of murder as impossible. Each time she'd met those black and white blue eyes in the photograph she had felt sure that what had appeared a great mystery at the time had eventually been happily resolved. Perhaps it had turned out to be a custody kidnapping, in which the abductive parent had proved more clever than most. She had firmly wrapped her speculations up with the peelings and deposited them in the bin. Still, that little persistent niggle of unease had led her to casually mention the matter to Aunt Jane over the beautifully scalloped potatoes at dinner, and they had both agreed that, given the vagueness of her impressions and the amount of time that had passed, the matter was purely academic anyway. There was no point in calling Aunt Jane's 'tame' policeman.

At first, Detective Hedges had been greatly entertained by the offer of 'psychic' help in tracking down a missing person, but it hadn't taken more than two or three direct hits for him to revise his thinking about the 'eccentric old biddy' who occasionally rang up and offered her services. Aunt Jane had been delighted to act as a conduit for information on those rare occasions that Seven couldn't avoid or ignore her perceived duty. While her aunt had revelled in her 'talented amateur detective' status and the publicity it generated, Seven had been only too pleased to hide behind her flamboyant notoriety. It was bad enough that sometimes her presentiments were too strong to be denied. To have to go through the infinitely wearisome trial by scorn each time it happened was more than she was willing to endure. So she used Aunt Jane and she could hardly object if she suspected her aunt—now and then when things were slow—of deliberately drawing her attention to some celebrated case or other in the hope that Seven might experience one of her 'brilliant insights', as the police coyly described her help.

'All right, I'll help,' Seven said finally now, with infinite weariness.

Aunt Jane clasped her hands together in an effort not to show too much unsightly glee. 'I knew you would! I knew you wouldn't say no. You won't regret it, Seven.' She beamed magnanimously.

'I'm regretting it already,' Seven replied wryly. At times Aunt Jane had the wisdom of Solomon, at others the rash, adventuresome naïveté of a child. Seven never knew which to expect.

'But no fuss, Aunt Jane. And no more talk of payment, whatever happens. I don't want That Man to have any more grounds for complaint.' Already he was assuming a capital importance in her life. Seven sighed. She needed no ESP to tell her that they were in for some turbulent times if Jake Jackson discovered that they had ignored his warnings. But she'd rather battle a flesh and blood man than implacable fate…at least against a man she had some chance of winning!

Two days later she reluctantly trailed her aunt into the large, sprawling, irregularly shaped cedar pentagon that was the Jackson home.

Charlotte Jackson was a surprise. Seven had expected someone a bit fluffy and frail and possibly neurotic, given her son's protective comments about her vulnerability. Instead she was a tall, thin, strong-looking woman who didn't look as though she needed anyone's protection. Certainly she seemed totally in control of herself and her life as she ushered her two visitors into a beautiful lounge overlooking the rear patio and the big fenced swimming-pool below it. The furnishings were in blue and grey, comfortable and modern, and the room had a lightly cluttered feel to it that bespoke a home rather than an expensive showcase.

Her handshake, when they were introduced, was firm and dry, and only when she drew away did Seven detect the faintest hint of a tremble in her fingertips. As they sat down on the blue parachute-silk couch Charlotte Jackson lit up a cigarette with a little self-conscious grimace that admitted her foolishness. For the rest of the visit she was never without one, although Seven noticed that she used them to gesture more than to puff on.

In her quiet grey suit Seven endeavoured to blend into the background as Charlotte Jackson talked about her granddaughter, the pain that sliced off her words palpable in the cool room.

'It's the not knowing that's the strain, you see. And the way that Rebecca's name has become an embarrassment. People just don't want to know any more. It's as if they felt a personal sense of failure about her disappearance, as if I'm criticising them by mentioning her. I think that's because there was so much publicity, you see. Oh, I understand Jake's motives at the time for trying to make everyone feel they had a responsibility for finding Becky and the man who took her, but it had its disadvantages. It's very difficult to keep up the faith when everyone around you is offering you pity and condolences because they believe the worst.' She lit another cigarette, the previous one stubbed out only half smoked. Of course it had been difficult for him, but at least he had his work to occupy him. From what she had said, Charlotte Jackson's whole reason for living had been the care and upbringing of her granddaughter.

'...Initially, of course, we expected a ransom or grudge note, but there was nothing. That was the first blow...' The taut voice faltered. Charlotte Jackson wasn't as much in control as she appeared. 'Waiting for the call that never came...hoping against hope it really was a kidnapping.' She caught Seven's shocked look and addressed her directly for the first time. 'A ransom demand would have given us a *reason*, a clue. If it wasn't a kidnapping then we had to accept it was something uglier, that some maniac had her... Jake's paper has covered this kind of story often enough for him to know that, the longer a child is missing, the more likely it is to be found dead. If it's a little girl and it's not for money or a grudge...well...' The blue eyes glittered with emotion and she had to take a sharp breath.

'The only sighting was by a young boy who wasn't very reliable—he couldn't even give a proper description of the man or the car that he claimed to have seen. The reward that we posted didn't help much either, it just encouraged the hoax calls. I can't tell you how many times we've had our hopes raised, only to find out it was someone out for the reward. But I couldn't give up hoping—I can't. Even crank calls were better than no calls at all. These last few years have been a long, unbearable silence. I don't want to forget. I mustn't. Jake thinks I'm mad, but he's given up, you see. He doesn't believe that Becky's still alive. He thinks something *ghastly* happened to her all those years ago. That she's buried somewhere, or in a river...otherwise *someone* would have seen her, a little girl who didn't belong wherever she was.' The rather stiff mouth trembled and Seven knew she was looking at a strong woman at the end of her tether. No wonder Jake Jackson was worried. So much pain clasped so fiercely for so long, something had to give some time. And the only thing holding Charlotte Jackson together at the moment, rightly or wrongly, was the slender thread of hope that Madame Zoe had held out. Even she admitted its foolishness, and yet was was incapable of denying it. Seven made up her mind, there and then, that if it was within her power she would bolster this woman's fading strength.

'What do the police think?' Seven asked.

'The case is still open.'

Such a bald statement, stark with fear.

'People try to pretend, for my sake, that it never happened. That Rebecca never even existed. Even Jake pretends. But I don't want pretence any more. She did exist and I want to affirm that. I want to *know*. That's all I ask now. Not to have her back. But just to know.' The truncated desire was a confession of utter despair.

'Know your future...find what has been lost.' The advertisement must have seemed like an omen, the answer to a prayer.

'Do you still have some of Rebecca's things?' Aunt Jane began, her previous eagerness muted by the other woman's suffering.

'Oh, her room is just the way it was when she disappeared. Jake wanted to pack away her clothes and toys but I wouldn't let him...I mean, that would have been admitting defeat, wouldn't it?' Charlotte Jackson rose, stubbing out her fourth cigarette. 'It's upstairs...we always used to worry about Rebecca on the stairs, but she was a great climber. She'd climb the gate that we fixed across them without a sign of fear and go up and down all day if we let her——'

Seven interrupted her rapid speech. 'Mrs Jackson, before we go any further—my aunt has decided that she doesn't want any payment for what she's doing.' There was an abrupt movement of protest in the corner of her vision that Seven resolutely ignored. 'If she can help, she will, but because she wants to, not for profit.'

'Oh, Madame Zoe!' The blue eyes flickered with relief as Charlotte Jackson grasped the now slightly sulky-looking Jane Selkirk's hand.

'And perhaps, since this isn't a professional engagement, you could call my aunt by her real name. She only uses Madame Zoe for business reasons, her name is actually Jane Selkirk.'

'So my son told me.' Charlotte Jackson's earlier stiffness had completely dissolved. She smiled warmly at her two visitors, giving Seven a glimpse of the woman she might have been six years ago, before tragedy had forced her emotions underground. 'I'm afraid he did his best to convince me that you were only after my money, but I'm glad I didn't take any notice. He'll have to eat his words now, won't he?'

'Can we see upstairs, now?' Aunt Jane asked abruptly, still struggling with the disappointment of being denied her due title on top of losing what she saw as her 'commission'. But she was too shrewd to protest out loud, and too wary of Seven in this mood of quiet determination.

'Of course...Jane. And do call me Charlotte. After all, we're going to be friends not business acquaintances. And...Seven? That's an unusual name.'

At least she hadn't said *odd*. 'I was born at seven minutes past seven in the morning of the seventh day of the seventh month, the seventh baby to be born at the hospital on that day. My mother was rather fanciful,' Seven explained with the speed of much repetition.

'Well, she could hardly ignore the omens, could she?' Charlotte smiled, leading the way up the wide carpeted stairs.

The child's room was a frozen frame of the past. The cot, a blanket drawn blindly up over the mattress, stood under the sloping window. There were colourful friezes and transfers on the plain cream walls and toys stacked neatly in a bright red toy box in the corner and displayed on top of a small bookcase filled with bright board books. On the wall above the cot there was a montage of photographs—Rebecca on a merry-go-round being held by her proud grandmother; Rebecca laughing on a swing; Rebecca crying on a slide; Rebecca asleep, blowing two candles out on a cake, pouting, laughing, living... It was a room filled with love and memories and Seven halted at the door. She didn't want to go in. She watched Charlotte Jackson point out Rebecca's favourite books and toys and listened to her talk in the relentless present tense about her granddaughter's sparkling personality. She could feel the tension in the room building up, like an invisible wall in front of her, a barrier that had to be broken through. And still she hesitated.

Charlotte turned around, as if she sensed Seven's reluctance, which verged on repulsion.

'I suppose a psychiatrist would say there was something wrong with me for keeping everything this way,' she said with a trace of desperation. 'And I suppose there is, in a way, because even if...when...we do find her she'll have grown out of all these toys and clothes. But I couldn't let her come back to nothing, could I...an empty room? She might need to know that we haven't forgotten...'

There was a moment of silence, then Jane drew herself up, remembering her role. 'Do you think I might have one of those pictures?' She pointed. 'It helps to have a strong visual image of the person we're looking for.'

'Of course.' As Charlotte hurried to comply Seven succumbed to the potent lure of her pain. She took a step, and another, feeling the atmosphere of the room close around her like the jaws of a trap. She drifted, for a moment, until the final shreds of resistance tore away, then was pulled over to stare down at the small, battered felt penguin that lay in the corner of the bare cot. It was like a hot-spot in the room. Even if she didn't want to see it, she could feel it. Seven had never been able to describe what she experienced in her moments of pre-cognition, had never wanted to. One could fight, one could accept, but one couldn't explain. Now she felt the inexplicable feelings intensify... not thought, but not emotion either, physical and yet remote from her body, gripping, frightening... There was always fear. Fear that one day she might step too far into the profound abyss of her ignorance. She knew something was waiting for her there in the blackness, some knowledge, something to hold on to... but what if in her blind, psychic fumbling she missed... and fell into the nothingness?

'That's Percy. Rebecca would never sleep without him,' said Charlotte in a stiff little voice. 'It's silly, but all I could think of at first was that they hadn't taken Percy, too. I would have felt better if they had. At least I'd have known that she had something loved and familiar to cling to. She always made a terrible fuss if we didn't tuck her up with Percy...'

Jane Selkirk made a sound of approval. 'That's just what we want—a possession with strong connections to the child.' She looked expectantly at Seven, who didn't move. Jane clicked her tongue impatiently and bent down to scoop up the penguin. As she did so there was the sound of a throaty growl in the driveway.

Charlotte hesitated, looking for a moment as if she would snatch the beloved penguin from Jane's grasp, then she hurried over to the window and looked down on to the driveway where it widened out to give access to the double garage beside the house.

'Oh, dear.' She turned, flustered. 'It's Jake. I was *sure* he wouldn't be home. Perhaps he's just calling in...if you could wait up here...?' She stopped, and pulled herself together, expelling a short breath of self-disgust. 'No, that's silly. He'll have to know...it may as well be now. I'm sorry, there'll probably be some unpleasantness, but it can't be avoided. Jake is...well...naturally rather overprotective where I'm concerned, but I want you to know that he does *not* run my life. He doesn't have to like what I'm doing, but he's not going to stop me, either.'

There came the distant slam of a door and clipped steps on the slate tiles which paved the entry below.

'It's only me!' The reassuring call floated up the stairs but the three women were far from reassured. Seven thought she had never met a man who was less entitled to lay claim to that self-effacing 'only'.

Charlotte paused at the door to light another cigarette. She hadn't reached for one the entire time they had been in her granddaughter's room, Seven realised, nor had she appeared to miss the prop. Consciously or subconsciously the small, pristine childish environment was considered sacrosanct against the invasion of life's grubby realities. A symbol of innocence in a world of pain.

At the top of the stairs they could see the man below, talking to a brisk, efficient-looking woman in an apron. The housekeeper, Seven guessed, instinctively dropping behind the other two, her palms dampening as she contemplated the moment of confrontation.

As Charlotte began to descend, Jane Selkirk suddenly turned with a violent tinkling of charms that caught the attention of those below, and thrust the shabby penguin into Seven's arms.

It was like being hit in the face with a cast-iron frying-pan. Seven's eyes flew wide, meeting the startled, then furious gaze of the man below, then her mind's defences ruthlessly slammed the lid on her consciousness. Without a sound she went down, the stairs rushing up to meet her as she crumpled gracelessly, gratefully, into the indigo darkness.

CHAPTER THREE

SEVEN came to consciousness slowly. There was something very soft beneath her, soft and smooth, and something warm over her, a feather-light weight that was barely there. She could feel the comforting caress of someone's breath on her forehead. Warily she opened her eyes.

Six inches away the indigo darkness loomed. Her lids snapped instantly shut.

'Come on, Miss Selkirk, I know you're in there. The voice was gravel over silk, redolent with a menacing impatience.

Her long silky brown lashes trembled and the delicate cheeks which had been porcelain-pale a few seconds before were awash with heat. It took all of her courage to obey the trenchant command. Her eyes opened again, her pupils huge and dark with dismay.

The warmth beneath her was the butter-smooth upholstery of a very luxurious leather couch. A soft mohair blanket was tucked around her, tickling her chin with its feathered fringe. And a breath away waited Jake Jackson, his arm braced across her body, his hard hip crowding her extended legs as he perched beside her slender length. The rest of his body was hard, too, coiled with tension, and the expression on his face was anything but sympathetic. His navy eyes had shaded towards the violent end of the spectrum and Seven shivered, going pale again.

'Are you all right, dear?' Aunt Jane appeared at his shoulder, but Seven couldn't take her eyes off the man holding her prisoner with his intensity.

'What's the matter, forgotten your lines?' he snapped as her tongue remained frozen to the roof of her mouth. 'You're supposed to say "what happened, where am I?" with just the right touch of dazed helplessness.'

'Jake!' His mother hovered anxiously on the other side of the couch. 'What a terrible thing to say. She's just had a bad fall.'

'Mmm. Broken any bones? Anything worth suing for?' And he ran his hand insolently over Seven's body under the blanket, his crocodile smile a parody of concern, and he watched her shrink back into the cushions.

'Jake!' Charlotte's voice rose sharply as she cast Seven a look of awkward apology.

'Well, it was rather a *timely* fall, wasn't it?' he said remorselessly, removing his hand but not his insolent stare. 'Very dramatic and perfectly staged to avoid a sticky moment. In fact I wouldn't be surprised if Miss Selkirk isn't going to suddenly find herself suffering from an attack of amnesia. What a pity you didn't manage to skittle your aunt as well—that would have solved all your problems!'

'Really, Mr Jackson, there's no need to be insulting!' Aunt Jane bristled with offended dignity.

'I would say there's every need. You obviously didn't take my previous warning seriously. That means you're either too thick-skinned, too stupid or too greedy to accept defeat. Or perhaps you hoped a suitably incapacitating accident would get the money out of me another way. Forget it. I'll call an ambulance for your bruised and battered body, Miss Selkirk, but I'm damned if I'll pay a cent towards your undoubtedly long and expensive convalescence.'

It was bad enough that he had thought she had deliberately thrown herself off the top of the stairs in a fit of cowardice, but then to imply an even grosser motive! Seven thrust away the blanket and attempted to rise.

'Get away from me,' she whispered croakily. 'Let me get up.' He didn't budge, his arm and body blocking her escape, smug in his masculine superiority. Seven's temper flared. 'Let me up, you big bully!' she snapped, pushing herself upright and swinging her elbow sharply across to punch into his side under his outstretched arm. He gave a startled cough and folded and she slithered off the couch and stood up. Too quickly, as it turned out.

Red spots danced in front of her eyes and she swayed, putting a hand up to her strangely light head.

'Jake, catch her, she's going to fall again!' Charlotte warned urgently, but her son merely stood, rubbing his side, watching her stagger.

Seven mistook his movement for compliance. She flinched. 'Don't you touch me,' she warned him thickly, a fierce light burning in her grey eyes, giving them the eerie yellow glow of a sky before a storm.

He held up his hands. 'I wouldn't dream of it,' he murmured drily, his brain beginning to function again as the clouds of fury dissipated. He had covered a few boxing matches in his time and he knew the signs of punch-drunkenness when he saw them. Whatever her intentions, little Miss Mouse had evidently taken a pounding. Her colour was all over the place and the pouty, fussy ruffles of her cream blouse were shaking with the effects of her quick, shallow breaths. As far as he could tell she hadn't hit her head when she fell, but she was only a tiny thing. Maybe she had a thin skull, as well as tissue-thin skin that showed every shift in blood flow.

'You'd better sit down before you fall down,' he told her.

'Go to hell!' She startled herself with her own vehemence.

A snarling mouse. In spite of himself he grinned and watched with interest as she tried to master her weaving limbs.

'Perhaps you'd better sit down, dear, until you feel better. You do look terribly pale.' Aunt Jane added her insistence. No doubt the worried expression on her face was quite genuine, but Seven knew that her fertile mind was probably working full bore on turning the unexpected situation to her best advantage.

'I'm perfectly all right.' To prove it she took a wobbly step.

'Oh, for God's sake!' Jake reached out and jerked her by the arm. She let out a shriek as she toppled and found herself plastered against his chest. He was wearing a suit but the jacket was open and through his thin shirt she could feel the crisp cushion of hair that contoured the sculpted muscle. Her thoughts skittered away and he took advantage of her distraction to dump her unceremoniously back on to the couch. She sat there stiffly, trying to recover her breath, a picture of outraged dignity. She tidied her hair and clothes while she recovered herself, conscious of the big oaf standing there, arms across his chest, enjoying his petty little victory.

'Why don't I get Mrs Taylor to make you a nice cup of tea?' Charlotte offered brightly. 'I'm sure you could do with one after your nasty shock.' She gave her son a look of stern disapproval which he shed with a cynical shrug.

'A slug of whisky would be more effective. I think I might even have one myself.'

They were in a big room she hadn't seen before, and Seven's mouth compressed with unconscious disapproval as she watched him go over to a well-stocked bar in the bookcase along one wall. A computer and printer occupied a big desk facing the full length windows that opened out on to the patio and, although there was the couch and two matching chairs, most of the room was purely utilitarian. His work-place, she guessed. It must be the room opening directly off the bottom of the stairs. Had she fallen the whole flight?

The drink he poured himself was large. He turned, holding the bottle, and held it up enquiringly.

'No, thank you,' she said primly, and his eyebrows rose scornfully as he detected her disapproval.

'Are you a prohibitionist, as well as a librarian, Miss Selkirk? Would you like to drain life of all its variety and colour? Do you consider it your duty to censor the books that go on your shelves? I bet you do. I bet you like your literature as artificially neat and tidy and bland as you are yourself.'

Seven blushed, not because he was right but because she was wrong. It was evening after all, and he'd just come in from a hard day's…muck-raking. He probably needed the drink—if only to wash the taste of the grubby stories he had edited out of his mouth! And what he did in the privacy of his own home was none of her business.

'I'll go and get Mrs Taylor to put the kettle on,' said Charlotte firmly, taking hold of the awkward moment. 'We'll have it in the lounge. We can all sit down and have a *civilised* discussion about this. You just rest for a few minutes,' she patted Seven's shoulder, 'and just come on through when you feel up to it. It's just next door.'

To Seven's horror her aunt sidled out after her hostess, making discreet kneading motions behind her back with her crabbed hands. Surely she didn't expect her niece to soften up a tough customer like Jake Jackson?

'Oh, but, Aunt Jane, we can't stay! We…I——'

'Have books to burn? Stills to smash?' suggested Jake Jackson smoothly, taking the chair opposite the couch, toasting her with his glass as she watched the two women depart with a wrinkled brow.

Seven nibbled her lower lip. 'Mr Jackson, I know you don't want us here——'

'How perceptive of you——'

'But I didn't fall down that staircase deliberately. I…I tripped.'

He took a healthy swallow of his drink, regarding her thoughtfully over the rim of his glass.

'I wonder why I don't believe you,' he murmured.

Because she was lying, that was why—trying not to think of what had caused her loss of consciousness, let alone talk about it. She lowered her eyes, nervously pleating her skirt with pale fingers. This man had made a career out of ferreting the truth out of people—and then slanting it to suit himself. Who knew what confidence-shattering technique he would spring on her next?

She cleared her throat. 'Your...your mother begged my aunt to come. She was upset——'

'And we both know why.'

Seven screwed up her courage, 'Yes, because of the way you acted——'

'Me!' The whisky slopped dangerously in his glass.

Seven gulped and continued doggedly on, 'Making her feel terrible about what she was doing. As if she didn't have any right to make her own decisions. Just because someone has different beliefs and aspirations from you it doesn't make them a fool whose needs should be ignored...' Her little burst of defiance faded out as he sneered openly.

'And what vast experience of human nature do you base this theory on, Miss Selkirk? A lifetime immured in the library service? How old are you? Thirty? Well, I'm thirty-six and I've seen a hell of a lot more of the world, and I *know* the damage half-baked theories like yours can cause——'

'I happen to be twenty-six!' huffed Seven, bristling.

'You look older,' he said, taking a drink. 'It must be the stagnating atmosphere that does it. Either that or the stress of trying to control that crazy old aunt of yours.'

'She's not crazy,' said Seven firmly. 'And the library does not stagnate...it's changing all the time to meet the needs of each new generation of readers. And for your information I happen to enjoy my career. It's very rewarding. At least what I do has a redeeming social value!'

'And you think that what I do hasn't?' he asked pleasantly and she bit her lip.

'I...I didn't say that.'

'You implied it.'

'Yes, well...' She looked away from those penetrating eyes.

'Come on, Miss Selkirk. Don't you even have the courage of your convictions? Professionally you may have something to boast about, but personally your ethics are shot to hell. After all your shocked protests here you are, perpetuating a cruel myth——'

He was goading her, she knew it, but she couldn't help saying tautly, 'I suppose it's only natural that a man who spends his days wallowing in swill becomes inured to the stench. That newspaper of yours has warped your thinking. In *your* world, everyone has a base motive for their actions. At least I have an open mind, Mr Jackson. *You* have an open sewer!' Ignoring her aches and pains, she jumped to her feet and he rose, too, dropping his empty glass carelessly on the floor between them as he blocked her passage to the door.

Seven's eyes widened with the tremendous effort of standing up to him. She didn't dare blink as he glared at her.

'Well, well...so the little mouse has teeth, and sharp ones at that. Maybe the little mouse is even a rat.'

'Takes one to know one,' said Seven sharply, and then flushed at her childish response. So much for impressing him with her intelligence! But the idea that he was thinking of her as a mouse was strangely hurtful. She knew that she wasn't a great beauty and that her personality didn't so much vibrate as gently hum, but not everyone was cut out to be bold and brilliant.

'It does at that.' He studied her flushed resentment and his brief flare of renewed anger died. He continued more mildly, 'So be warned. And be sensible—stay out of my way. Don't let yourself be bullied into doing anything stupid.'

Her chin lifted in defiance at the slur. 'Unlike your mother, I'm allowed to make my own decisions. Nobody bullies me into doing anything I don't want to do,' she said truthfully, thinking of the core of bedrock stubbornness that shocked people who thought that because she wasn't brashly confident she was a push-over. For good measure she added, 'Not even you.'

'No?' He leaned closer, right into her face, and growled suddenly, a deep rusty sound that rattled her bones. She took a hasty step back, startled, and he laughed. 'Little mouse. You're scared of your own shadow.'

'That isn't what you thought a few moments ago.' She stood her failing ground. She'd almost rather be thought a dyed-in-the-wool villainness than a spineless doormat.

'A few moments ago you weren't. Are you a head librarian?'

Seven was taken aback by the change of subject. 'Yes,' she admitted carefully, looking for the catch.

He smiled as if she had told a joke. 'A woman of unlimited power in her own little domain.'

'I happen to be very good at my job,' said Seven stiffly. He seemed to find her career funny, when in reality it was very fulfilling.

'I didn't say you weren't. I must come and see you some day. Which branch are you in? Perhaps I'll come and apply for a card.'

Seven looked at him in horror. For some reason the idea of him invading the peace of the St Thomas's Library was unthinkable. She had never been one of those psychics who claimed to have seen 'auras' surrounding people—that was her aunt's fantasy—but she had no difficulty imagining this man enclosed in a crackling field of blue-white static electricity. It interfered with her concentration, the messages her brain was interpreting from her body. She would find it difficult to think straight around him, let alone concentrate on work.

'I feel better now. I think I——'

'I can find out, you know. You'd be surprised at the sources I have.'

'Oh, no, I wouldn't,' she murmured. He would leave no stone unturned in his quest for a juicy story. What if he came and made a fuss about Aunt Jane at the library? She would hate that even more than the publicity of a court case. The library was her haven of orderly normality. 'I really must go.'

She ducked around him and hurried out to chivvy her aunt.

'But my mother invited us to have a civilised talk, remember?' The devil spoke in her ear, close on her heels. 'Can't you trust yourself to be civilised around me, little mouse?'

The short answer was no. 'Stop calling me that!'

'I refuse to keep calling you Miss Selkirk. Surely such polite formality is redundant in our case.'

'Politeness is never redundant,' said Seven primly. 'I happen to think that a little more polite formality in the world might solve a lot of its problems.'

'You would,' he muttered as they entered the lounge where Charlotte and Jane had their heads together over bone china cups. They were talking in low, intense tones and broke off abruptly at the interruption. Aunt Jane began ladling sugar into her cup as Charlotte's eyes moved from her son's suspicion to Seven's agitation. What was going on? Aunt Jane *never* took sugar in her tea.

'Milk or lemon, Seven?' Charlotte asked as her hand hovered over the silver teapot.

'Seven?' Jake jerked out. *'Seven?'* There was a shock of laughter in his voice as he turned to look at her. 'You have a number rather than a name? Do you use the Dewey system to classify people, as well as the books in your life? I wonder what classification *seven* denotes— fiction, perhaps? Science fiction? Fables? Moral tales?'

'Jake, it's not very pleasant to make jokes about people's names. It wasn't her choice after all, but I happen to think it's very distinctive and attractive.' Charlotte sprang to her defence with commendable speed. 'Don't you take any notice of him, Seven, he's never quite got over the fact that we christened him John. It's so ordinary, you see, and even as a child Jake was convinced that he was destined for extraordinary things. When he was seven he announced that he was going to answer to J.J. and nothing else, but his father put his foot down. James said that no son of his was going to hide behind a set of coy initials, however distinctive. So we settled on Jake, didn't we, dear, as a compromise— because even then you were such an awfully pugnacious little boy. Although I notice that his employees all call him J.J. So, you see, he did get his own way in the end.' She sighed, as if it was something she was long resigned to. Sensing that her son didn't appreciate having his childish foibles trotted out in the present company, his mother hurried to explain how Seven had got her unusual name.

Now it was Seven's time to squirm.

'Funny. I had you pegged as an Abigail, or Mabel, or possibly Victoria.' His voice was threaded with his former contempt.

'Well, that just goes to show that you're not *always* right,' she pointed out quietly.

'I freely admit it. But when I'm wrong I like to know why, and how. I don't just back off wringing my hands. I get the facts and try again.' It was an oblique threat that only Seven seemed to register.

'To bend them to fit your theory,' she said, her eyes chilly with disdain.

His face hardened, but to her dismay he didn't attempt to deny it. He just stood there, big and bold, daring her to take the issue further. Heavens, here she was a guest in his home, and an unwelcome one at that, and she was lecturing him pompously on manners and ethics. She had fiercely resented him storming into her home reeking contempt, but she was no better.

'I'm sorry...' she said, hating to apologise but compelled to by her own inbred good manners. Her aunt had wanted her to placate him and all she had done was stir him up with her antagonism. 'I...shouldn't have said that.'

'Why not, if that's your opinion?' He was giving no quarter.

'I...it was very rude.'

'But I was being very provoking.'

'Oh, no! Yes—that is...I'm sure you...you...'

'Weren't doing it on purpose?' He cocked his head, his eyes slitting to hide a gleam of what might have been humour.

They both knew very well that he had been purposely goading her, but politeness demanded she accept the proffered olive-branch. 'Yes! I'm sure you didn't mean to...to...'

'Call you a cheat and a liar and a woman of no heart and less morals——'

'Jake!'

Seven bit her lower lip. Hard. Beast! She felt herself blushing, even though Charlotte's censorious eyes were on her son. As for Aunt Jane! How could she sit there meekly stirring her revoltingly sweet tea and looking like a perfectly innocent, uninvolved stranger? Seven sucked her bruised lip soothingly. It would probably be the size of a plum by the time she got home. She ran her tongue experimentally over the slight swelling there and suddenly noticed that Jake was watching. Having him staring at her mouth gave her a funny, prickly feeling up the back of her skull. She pressed her lips together primly and his eyes shot up and the prickly feeling got worse. She felt hot and flustered and was sure that her bun was drifting apart. Her comfortable wool gabardine suit felt tight and wrinkled. Heaven knew what she had shown off when she'd tumbled down those stairs. Had he discovered that she was wearing stockings rather than tights, held up with a lavender lace suspender belt that had been a sinful extravagance? Was that why there was suddenly a very knowing look in those navy eyes? Seven was in an agony of confusion.

'I don't think I'll have any tea, thank you, Mrs—Charlotte. We really must be going...'

To her relief Aunt Jane came out of her innocent abstraction without demur. She checked the tiny gold watch that was attached to the charm bracelet, squinting at the almost illegible figures. 'Oh, goodness, yes. I have a seance to prepare for...'

'Oh?' It was obviously on the tip of Charlotte's tongue to ask a slew of questions but one thunderously quelling look from her son and she subsided into her teacup. 'Ah, well, if you must go. Are you sure you're all right, Seven? Perhaps I'd better check that carpeting at the top of the stairs. If Jake hadn't leapt up the stairs to catch you, you might have suffered a serious injury.'

Jake had caught her? Oh, dear...

'I didn't realise. Th...thank you.' The words stuck awkwardly in her throat and came out in a husky whisper.

'It was my pleasure, Seven,' he replied politely, instilling his limpid gaze with all sorts of lacivious suggestions as to why it had been such a pleasure. The cruel humour surfaced completely when she reacted with typical sensitivity and blushed furiously.

If Seven didn't escape she was going to suffer a total meltdown. The man was insufferable. He even turned her honest, abject apologies against her—a lion taunting a mouse. At least, though, she had provided a distraction to keep his big paws off her aunt.

'I'll be in touch,' said Charlotte, lighting another cigarette before she rose to confront her son's anger.

'Don't bank on it,' he said grimly. 'If I see either of you two on this property again I'll have you arrested for trespass, and that'll only be the beginning of the charges,' he told Jane Selkirk, who, with her usual unconcern for practical reality, merely smiled vaguely. Part of that vagueness was a protective veneer, Seven knew, but Aunt Jane also possessed a genuine imperviousness to hostility that bordered on the dangerous. Jake seemed to recognise it because he turned to Seven with a grunt of frustration. 'You tell her.'

'I think you've made your feelings perfectly clear to everyone, Mr Jackson——'

'And so have I,' said Charlotte, puffing furiously. 'If they can't come here, well—I'll just have to go there. No, Jake——' at his violent movement '—this time I won't be stopped. I'm not a child to be protected from myself. I don't need your permission. If you don't approve you don't have to be involved...in fact I'm asking you not to be. I'll do this by myself. I don't ask much of you, do I, Jake? You live your own life how you please, you always have. All I ask is that I be allowed to do the same!'

His frustration was an intangible, writhing presence in the room as his mother marched past him, her arm tucked firmly under Jane's. For a few seconds after they left the room Seven hovered uncertainly.

'What did she mean...this time?'

'You don't think this is the first time I've had to play the heavy with the lunatic fringe?' he growled savagely. 'Every year on the anniversary of Rebecca's disappearance we go through the same damned trauma. Two years ago they even came up with a live candidate!'

'You mean, a suspect?'

'I mean a victim. A couple claimed to have found Rebecca. They even had a fake locket made, from the pictures circulated at the time. Oh, they had their story down pat, but unfortunately they couldn't fake the child's X-rays. Rebecca had an unusual bone formation that just wasn't there. Mother was all prepared to welcome them with open arms—and cheque-book. It totally devastated her for months. Almost wrecked her health.'

'My God!' Seven was unutterably appalled, suddenly understanding the rooted depths of his violent objection. 'I had no idea...I'm so sorry——'

'Sorry enough to stop this putrid farce?' he demanded savagely.

'I'll do my best,' she vowed gently. And she would. If she could find out something about the fate of his daughter she could put an end to his mental agony for once and for all. No more farces. No more ugly annual memorials. She touched his arm, feeling some of the warmth of her certainty flow into the frozen rigidity of his body.

He looked at her, his eyes narrowing as he shook off her unsettling touch, massaging his tingling arm, wondering where the helpless black rage had gone. With her pale hand and soft voice she had soaked it up like blotting paper and left in its place a kind of emptiness that begged to be filled.

'What is it about you, mouse, that makes me want to either stroke you or strangle you, sometimes simultaneously? No—don't shy away.' He cupped a big hand around her hot cheek, his thumb moving over her fragile bones. He could hurt her so easily, and it shocked him to the core that the knowledge was actually arousing him. Then he realised that it wasn't the concept of causing her pain that aroused him, but the thought that he couldn't... that he would have to handle her very delicately, very slowly, very surely—with a gentleness that would be a challenge to his arrogant masculinity. She would shatter in his hands if he gave her more pleasure than the shy little body could cope with all at once. He would have to take his time, build her trust slowly...

My God, what was he thinking of? Jake snatched his hand away in disgust, clenching it by his side to distract himself from the aching fullness in his loins.

'If you hurt her, so help me——' he began harshly.

'I know,' she said gravely, sensing a new source for his anger but unable to pin-point it. Well, she never claimed to be able to read minds!

'Can I trust you? I must be mad to even contemplate it. I'll be behind you, you know, every step of the way.' And what an enticing prospect *that* was! He must have really degenerated socially over the past few years to find anything sexually exciting about a musty librarian with the social sophistication of a hedgehog and the body of a jockey. Jake enjoyed women who were gregarious and *built*.

She had obviously imagined that hungry look in Jake Jackson's eye, thought Seven, as she drove her aunt home in the ageing, but beautifully cared for Honda Civic that was her pride and joy. It was ridiculous to kid herself that a man like him would find her attractive, except as a joke. No, he had probably been hungering for her blood, rather than her body...

'Well, I think that turned out rather well, don't you?'

Seven looked at her aunt in disbelief. 'How can you say that? He practically threw us out!'

'Yes, but not before I got everything settled with Charlotte. He'll come around, you'll see. The sceptics are always the hardest to fall.'

'You mean the hardest, to *fell*,' muttered Seven, her eye falling on her aunt's suspiciously bulging macrame bag. Her 'bag of tricks'. 'What have you got there? You didn't take anything, did you?' In her present state, Seven was prepared for the worst.

'Of course not!' her aunt snapped. 'Why, that would be theft. No—I have here the answer to all our problems!' A tall order, in the circumstances, Seven thought grimly, and then swerved wildly as Aunt Jane rummaged in her bag and produced a love-battered toy which she dangled in front of her niece's eyes.

'See—Percy Penguin!'

They were extremely lucky, Seven told her furiously later, that there hadn't been a lamppost at the kerbside. If there had been it wouldn't have just been a crumpled tyre-rim they'd have been dealing with. Aunt Jane might well have found herself conducting that night's seance from the 'other' side!

CHAPTER FOUR

'MISS SELKIRK, there's a man here to see you.'

'Oh?' Seven looked up at her most junior librarian, alerted by her breathless delivery.

'Yes. A reporter!' Cilla announced with feverish delight. She loved to dramatise herself, that much was obvious from the colourfully mismatched clothes she wore and the hair which varied in colour from day to day according to which hairspray she used. Whatever she was holding back was giving her full scope for her dramatic talents. She looked expectantly from Seven to the other occupant of the small office, Brad Stevens, who was working on a damaged book at his desk in the corner.

'Really.' Seven disappointed her with a calm reply, and then relented by adding, 'I wonder what he wants. Perhaps he's interested in the new Children's Story Hour.' The local paper had always been helpful in publicising the library's programmes.'

Cilla giggled, shaking her pink-streaked blonde locks. 'I doubt it, it's not that kind of paper—unless there's something kinky involved!'

Seven's stomach swooped.

'He's from that awful one...you know, the *Clarion*, the one that's being sued all the time,' Cilla went on, chagrined at the lack of response. 'You know, Miss Selkirk, the one that had that story last week about the Cabinet Minister who had two——'

'I can't imagine what he wants here,' Seven cut her off with the hopeful lie. Surely, surely Jake Jackson hadn't set his hounds on to the story already. 'Tell him

I'm—no——' She'd better be careful. 'Apologise and ask him if he can come back another time. I'm just too busy to see him at the moment.' An employee of the *Clarion* was probably immune to polite requests, but she might be able to fob him off at least until she had spoken to her aunt. Her thoughts congealed... unless he had *already* spoken to Aunt Jane and the old lady had been her usual confiding self.

'Do you want me to ask him what it's about?'

'No! Er, no.' Seven tempered her horrified cry with a weak smile. 'Just ask if it is convenient for him to come back. Perhaps he could ring first.' She wondered who Jake Jackson had sent to carry out his revenge—probably some rat-faced weasel whose mere presence would be an intrusive offence.

Seven dialled the house while Cilla was gone, but wasn't really surprised when the phone rang un-answered. On Wednesday mornings Aunt Jane went to the neighbourhood bridge club, not to play but to do tarot readings afterwards for the ladies, for which she was paid in home baking. They always had a treat for dessert on Wednesday nights.

Cilla was back, more breathless than ever, her cheeks flushed almost the colour of the streaks in her hair.

'He says it's most certainly not convenient. He says that if he can't talk to you he'll have to use his initiative and ask questions around the library—about you. He thinks you might prefer to answer them yourself. I don't think he's going to go away quietly, Miss Selkirk,' she added her own opinion to the ominous litany of quotes, trying to look regretful but not quite succeeding. Even Brad, a largely self-absorbed young man, was beginning to look intrigued.

Seven would have liked to hide under her desk, but a head librarian couldn't do anything so undignified. Instead she rose and automatically smoothed down her

skirt with a nervous hand. She squared her slim shoulders
and walked steadily out into the fray.

St Thomas's Library was one of the oldest in
Auckland, but the gothic-inspired architecture had lent
itself to modern renovation surprisingly well. Seven felt
possessively proud of her library, a nice compromise of
tradition and modern practicality that was graceful and
yet functional.

'He's over by the issue and return desk, Miss Selkirk,'
said Cilla, skipping excitedly at her heels.

Seven veered around the magazine display shelving and
headed towards the main desk which ran at right angles
to the library entrance.

'I wonder why he wants *you*, Miss Selkirk,' Cilla continued with irrepressible interest. 'I mean . . . a paper like
that. Were you a witness to something, Miss
Selkirk—— ?'

'This reporter,' interrupted Seven hastily. 'Did he give
you his name?'

'No, but he had a Press card. He—oh, there he is! Bit
of a hunk for an old guy, huh?'

Bit? Jake Jackson wasn't a *bit* of anything, he was
the complete appalling whole. Seven's mouth went dry
as she saw his expression. He wasn't a *bit* angry, either.

'M . . . Mr Jackson.' She'd have preferred a rat-faced
weasel.

'Miss Selkirk.' He was wearing a dark blue suit with
a blue and white striped shirt and a grey and maroon
tie and his formality was nearly as daunting as his
expression. 'You look surprised to see me. You shouldn't
be.'

'Do you know him, Miss Selkirk?' whispered Cilla in
her ear.

Seven smoothed back her hair and discovered she was
still wearing the tortoiseshell spectacles she wore for close
work. She snatched them off and cleared her throat.

'Mr Jackson——'

'You've said that once already. I know who *I* am. But what the hell are you?'

'I. . .?' Had he found out the truth? 'Mr——' she stopped herself just in time. 'Look, I'm fairly busy right now. Do you think that we could perhaps have this discussion at a more suitable time and place?'

'Interview, not discussion,' he corrected her roughly and she blanched. 'I think the time and the place are perfectly suitable, since there seems to be a vast gap between what you *say* in private and what you *do* in public. Let's try to reconcile the two for once, shall we? Do you recognise this?' He held out a piece of paper towards her.

Seven didn't even glance at it, trying to keep her chin up and her gaze as steady and as authoritative as she could as she replied quietly, 'Will you please keep your voice down, Mr Jackson? This is a library——'

'I said, do you recognise this?' He held the paper higher, and his voice rose commensurably. Heads lifted. A high school study group at one of the large tables began to whisper.

Seven felt her confidence waver. This was her realm, she reminded herself. She was in charge here, not him. 'If you're going to be difficult, Mr Jackson, then perhaps you had better come into my office.' She turned briskly away.

'No.' The negative bullet struck her square in the back. She froze.

'No?' She turned slowly to face the unwelcome challenge of his navy eyes.

'Here. Now,' he ordered in a raw voice that warned her not to take up the challenge. 'I'm not moving until you've answered my questions. For the record.' He tapped his jacket pocket and she noticed the rectangular bulge. A tape-recorder?

Seven heard a gasp behind her. Cilla was practically exploding with curiosity. 'Cilla, have you finished that reshelving you were doing?'

'Yes... almost,' the girl admitted reluctantly.

'Well, you'd better go and finish it, then.'

'Oh, but——'

'Now.' Seven wasn't aware that the command came out in exactly the same warning tone that Jake Jackson had used, but he was. He smiled grimly, without a lick of amusement.

'I thought perhaps, Mr... er... you might like a cup of coffee?' Cilla turned her cheeky charm hopefully on to the secondary object of curiosity.

'He's not thirsty. And he's not going to be here long enough to drink one. Please go and do that reshelving.'

Cilla retreated, oozing resentment, and Seven wasn't surprised to see her reappear a few minutes later working at the shelf closest to the issues desk. By that time, though, Seven had too many other things to worry about.

'How dare you come in here and disrupt my staff?' Seven hissed at the cause of her upset.

'You're the one causing the disruption. All I did was ask a simple question which you're still trying to evade answering. I don't care who else knows about this. But you obviously do. If you don't want it broadcast I suggest you co-operate.' His voice rang clear and bold in spite of the cleverly depressive library acoustics. More whispers and curious glances.

Seven took a steadying breath and snatched the paper out of his hand.

'It's only a photocopy. The police have the original. But then, you know that, don't you?'

She had to put her glasses back on to see the image clearly but she needn't have bothered. She had suddenly realised what it was that had provoked his appearance.

'Oh.'

'Yes. Oh,' he said grimly. 'Pretty, isn't it? Not bad for an old lady who modestly disclaims any artistic talent. But then I understand that she didn't actually draw it herself...it just "developed" on the paper under her hand.'

Seven sighed. 'Look, Mr Jackson——'

'I'm getting rather tired of that phrase. Why don't you skip the stuffy formality and call me Jake? Or J.J. if you prefer, since this is in the nature of a professional visit.'

'Perhaps I'll call you John,' she replied tartly. 'That is your name, isn't it, and not those glamorous aliases?'

His mouth twitched, but whether out of humour or annoyance she wasn't given time to determine. 'Tell me about the picture.'

'You seem to know all about it already——' she hedged.

'Seven!'

'I...that is, it's a house associated in some way with your...with Rebecca,' she said, her hand tightening on the sketch that she had drawn at midnight a week ago. 'It has very strong connections. My aunt borrowed Rebecca's favourite toy and it caused some very vivid dreams——' More in the nature of nightmares, a series of disconnected images that had been profoundly disturbing.

'My God, dreams! You really can't believe this!' he burst out. 'Dammit, you said you were going to help and you let this happen. I should have known better than to think you had any influence over that crazy woman. She should be in a damned institution, not running around loose. And to actually send the bloody thing to the police!'

He was working himself up to a booming temper and Seven couldn't do a thing about it. Everyone else in the library had stopped what they were doing and were entranced by the action. Making her decision, Seven folded the picture in her hands, took off her spectacles, and walked away, cheeks flaming. She got as far as her office before he came after her, with a roar.

'Don't you *ever* walk away from me.' His shock at having his temper ignored told her a lot. He must be a tiger in the newsroom.

'I'm sorry, I've read that that's the only way to treat a tantrum,' she said, elated by her own audacity. 'Brad, will you forgive us if we use the office for a while? Mr Jackson needs to cool down.'

'Uh, sure.' Brad gave the angry man an uncertain look. Seven knew what he was thinking.

'It's all right. He won't hurt me.'

There was a brief, uneasy silence. Then Jake swore with a black proficiency. 'Of course I won't damned well hurt her.'

'And if you wouldn't mind curbing your language.' As Brad hastily removed himself, Seven played on her unexpected advantage. 'It may be appropriate for your newsroom—and even your newspaper—but it's not for a library. We have children in here, and people who have more respect for the English language.'

He gritted his teeth audibly. 'My God, you're an irritating woman. Soft as butter and just as slippery.'

'A buttered mouse. You do love your hackneyed similes, don't you, J-Jake?' Just in time she stopped herself calling him John. She sensed that would be overstepping the mark.

Expecting a quick retaliation, she was unnerved when he said nothing. He looked at her through narrowed eyes, then around the room. He selected the chair beside her desk and sat down on it. He folded his arms behind his head and leaned back, stretching out his long legs. One beautifully crafted Italian leather shoe lifted to heel carelessly on to a pile of papers behind her computer screen, and the other stacked comfortably on top of it. Seven frowned with distaste at the picture of casual

belonging he presented. The sides of his jacket fell away
from his chest and his tie had slipped to one side. Seven
could see the dark shadow of chest hair through the pale
shirt. She remembered how soft and resilient that bed
of hair had felt against her breasts when he had held her
at his house. If their upper bodies had been bare it would
have felt even nicer. She wondered if he was as hairy all
over.

Her eyes shot to his, shocked by how far her thoughts
had wandered, and she blushed to find him studying her
with the same intensity. She was glad that her winter-
weight cardigan-jacket was fastened over her pale yellow
blouse, and that her fawn skirt was a respectable length.

'Could you please take your feet off my desk?' she
said sternly, hoping he would take her blush for one of
anger.

'Very brave, aren't you, in your head librarian's
shoes?' he said, not moving.

She ignored the perceptive taunt as she tried to ignore
her sudden awareness of his sex appeal. How dared he
manage to look so at home here, in her pleasant haven
of orderliness?

'You are a very rude man,' she told him tightly.

'I know.' He seemed unashamed of the accusation. 'I
certainly didn't get where I am today by accepting a load
of bull just because it's polite not to disagree. I say what
I think. And I think you're trying to give me the run-
around.'

Seven looked down at the folded paper on her desk
and unfolded it, putting on her spectacles again and pre-
tending to study it. Her hands felt icy and the familiar
pen-strokes danced before her eyes, inviting her back
into the nightmare. She pushed it away, shuddering.

'Did your mother give you this? I thought you weren't
going to involve yourself——'

'Those were my mother's words, not mine. And I can't
not be involved when I get a call from a police detective

asking my opinion.' Suddenly the vision of casualness vanished as he whipped his feet off the table and replaced them with a slamming fist that made Seven jump. 'Do you know what a sieve a police station is? Every cop on the block is going to know about it. It's going to be the joke of the force. And jokes that good get told around! How long do you think it's going to be before some hot-shot reporter hears about it and puts the joke on the wire?'

'I thought you didn't care about the publicity,' said Seven faintly.

'Not when I'm managing it, no!'

'Isn't that a bit hypocritical——?'

'Spare me the lectures. Just tell me what this new angle is.'

'It isn't an angle——'

'You know my mother has given your aunt a cheque——'

Seven could feel the perspiration on her brow. 'No, I didn't——'

'Expenses.' He spat the word out like rotten fruit. 'I run a newspaper, I know all the expenses fiddles there are, but this one takes the cake. Mileage charged on that gas-guzzler of yours. Apparently your aunt has been driving around looking for that mirage she drew. Very clever. Invent a non-existent place and then look for it.'

No wonder her aunt had offered to drive Seven to work for the last few days so that she could have the car to go to her various appointments. It had never occurred to Seven to check the mileage. Her eyes darkened with her angry thoughts. Thank goodness she had brought the car with her today. 'I...I'll make sure that the cheque is returned——'

'It's already been cashed.'

'The money, then. In fact I can give you a cheque now.' She pulled open the drawer where she kept her handbag during working hours. 'How much was it for?' she demanded, her pen poised for action.

'You tell me.'

'I beg your pardon?'

'Isn't that your speciality?'

She looked at him blankly. 'I don't understand.'

'I'm thinking of the amount. I'm concentrating on the figure.' He lifted his hands to his head, placing blunt fingers against his temples. 'I have a picture in my mind...' He went on with the whole ridiculous spiel. Not exactly the one that she and Morgan had learned to use in their act, but close enough to make her cringe.

'Did you think I wouldn't find out?' he taunted her pale dismay. 'The fact that I haven't published anything... *yet*, doesn't mean I haven't started to investigate. When I dig, I like to dig deep, because that's usually where the bones are buried.'

Seven struggled to regain her composure. 'I haven't got anything to hide,' she lied shakily. 'I haven't done anything to be ashamed of.'

'But you don't like to talk about it. I bet no one here knows that you have sawdust in your veins. The quiet and prim Miss Selkirk, council librarian, a circus performer of wide renown. You got quite a bit of Press coverage in those days.'

'I was only a child. It was a long time ago. I doubt that anyone would be interested after all this time——'

'I was. I found it fascinating. And enlightening. Did you coach your aunt in all the little tricks of the trade so you could experience of few of the old thrills from the vicarious safety of the sidelines——?'

'No!'

'Now I know why you're so tolerant of Madame Zoe's craziness...that was something I couldn't understand— a conventional, upright citizen like yourself condoning the activities of a borderline criminal. But, hey, all she's doing is continuing a family tradition, right?'

'That was different——'

'Yes, it was. In your case people *expected* to be conned. The Big Top invites a suspension of disbelief. But here in the real world the spangles don't hide the squalor. People don't laugh when they find out they've been tricked. *I'm* not laughing...'

'How much was the cheque for?' asked Seven stiffly, hiding her hurt behind the tatters of her dignity as she bent her head.

He let her write it with jerky slashes that revealed her inner turmoil. When she held it out to him he took it and tore it ragged across the middle, throwing the pieces back at her.

'I told you once before, I can't be bought off. Your aunt wanted to involve the police? Well, she might find that she'll get more than she bargained for. I haven't finished my digging yet, but when I do the hole's going to be big enough to bury both of you!'

Seven managed to control herself until he had stormed out, then she shut herself in the small staff bathroom and burst into a flood of tears. She couldn't remember the last time she had cried, and as the tears flowed she was amazed at how much they eased the suffocating tightness in her chest. It made her realise how used she had become to bottling up her feelings. She wasn't a strong person by nature, but these last few years she had had to shape herself into the semblance of one to cope with the changes in Aunt Jane and her unexpected promotion to head librarian. As her responsibilities had widened her personal choices had narrowed. Where were her friends? She had plenty of acquaintances but no one close enough to trust with her guilty secrets. And what about love? Most of the men she had dated she had met through work, and they tended to be serious, intellectual types who were attracted by her shy smile and quiet competence. She couldn't imagine any of them offering her a shoulder to cry on, or encouraging her to tell them what she really *felt* as opposed to what she *thought* ...

She stayed in the bathroom until she couldn't avoid her responsibilities any longer. She looked at herself in the mirror before she left and was shocked at her reflection. She looked so young and ... *distraught*. She tucked back the wisps of hair that had sprung out from her neat chignon and wished she had remembered to grab her bag before she had fled so that she could smooth some foundation over her flushed cheeks. Unfortunately her glasses could not disguise her swollen eyes, and she was resigned to her colleagues' avid curiosity as she stiffly made her way back to her desk. Surprisingly, neither Cilla nor Brad were hovering around the office.

Jake Jackson, however, was.

Seven took one horrified look at him and turned tail. It only took him two strides to catch up with her, knocking over a stack of uncatalogued books as he reached for her elbow to swing her around.

'Let go of me,' she demanded wretchedly, looking down at his Italian shoes, hoping her thick lashes would screen the pink rims of her eyes. It was a vain hope.

'You've been crying.' He sounded ridiculously shocked, considering the savage way he had carried on.

She debated denying it, but she was tired of fighting, of being torn by her emotions. 'Did you come back to gloat?'

There was a small, unrevealing silence. Seven resisted the fierce temptation to look at him. 'No. I got carried away back there. I have a brute of a temper sometimes. I came back to apologise.'

She couldn't help it then. She stared at him in disbelief. He met her gaze unflinchingly, the lack of hostility as alarming as the curiosity she saw nestling there. She looked away. She laughed nervously. She looked back, nibbling her lip. He was still watching her with that dark, unblinking gaze. She smoothed her skirt. She cleared her throat. She adjusted her spectacles. He reached into the inner pocket of his jacket and handed her a small tortoiseshell comb.

'What's that for?' she was startled into asking, looking at it as if he had offered her a snake, and a venomous one at that.

'To fuss with. You're running out of excuses not to speak. Am I really so disconcerting?'

'When you apologise, yes!' she flared, disdaining his comb. 'Does that mean that you take it all back?'

'No. Just the part where I attacked you for something you weren't responsible for—the circumstances of your childhood. Children are very vulnerable to the adult forces that shape their lives——'

'Thank you for that stunning insight, Dr Freud——'

'Now don't get defensive on me, Seven, I'm trying to understand——'

'I don't happen to want your understanding. It's not important to me——'

'Important enough to make the stiff-upper-lipped iron maiden of the library cry,' he said quietly.

It stopped her dead. She started to nibble her lip again, and he sighed and held up his comb once more. Seven pulled herself together. 'I have work to do——'

'No, you don't. Your assistant told me that you're overdue for your lunch break. Do you brown-bag, or go out?'

'I bring sandwiches,' she said automatically. 'I go to the park across the street.'

'Suits me.'

It didn't suit Seven, not at all. Yet ten minutes later they were sharing a sunlit park bench and he was eating the lion's share of her lunch while engaging her in desultory, neutral conversation.

'Mmm, delicious.' He swallowed the last crumb of his second sandwich. 'Any more?'

Seven's fingers tightened around her remaining sandwich and she took a hurried bite. 'No!' He sighed and she relented, only because she wasn't very hungry herself. 'There's an apple, if you want it.'

'Thanks.' He helped himself from the paper bag on her lap, screwing up the empty bag and rising to aim it at, and miss, the rubbish bin on the other side of the red gravel path. He got up and retrieved the bag, batting it into the bin. 'Never was much of a basketball player.' He half grinned at her as he sat down again and crunched into the crisp, glossy fruit.

'I suppose you played rugby at school,' said Seven, basing her judgement on his size...and his temperament!

'Gymnastics, actually,' he said, reading her with little effort. 'Strength and precision—the combination appealed to me. And the fact that it's a solo sport. I was never much of a team player. What about you?'

She chewed, not wanting to answer.

'Let me guess,' he murmured, hiding his smile behind the apple. 'You must have been very small and light. I would say...gymnastics?' His smile crept around the apple at her stubborn silence. 'Mmm...I wonder what else we have in common.'

One of the children who had been playing on the swings in the far corner of the small, grassy park chased a flock of sparrows over the small knoll in front of them. It was a little blonde girl of about four, dressed in a red parka that matched her rosy cheeks. Seven, her attention momentarily diverted, drew a sharp breath when her eyes swung back to Jake. His face was a collection of rigid angles, his eyes cold and empty as they followed the progress of the laughing, leaping child.

'Mr Jackson? Jake——?' Seven touched his arm, a little frightened by his utter stillness. 'Jake, are you all right?'

He shook his head sharply. 'Fine. I'm fine.' But it came out thick and rasping, his breathing out of sync with his voice, and his eyes were almost black with memories.

'It . . . must be very hard . . .' murmured Seven gently, unable to let him bear such pain alone.

A little colour seeped back into his face, his iron muscles relaxing a little under her hand. 'Sometimes . . . I'm usually prepared, but sometimes it just . . . sneaks up on me.'

'Did you ever think——? Do you think that you might ever want another child?'

He looked at her, as shocked as she by the intensely personal nature of her curiosity. 'The question doesn't arise,' he said in a bleak tone that closed the subject. Did that mean he avoided women who wanted children? That he never expected to marry again?

'Eat the rest of your apple.' She gently shook him out of his abstraction with her prosaic remark. 'It'll go brown and be wasted if you don't.'

'Would you like a bite?' He held it up to her lips, tempting and juicy. 'I'd hate to think I was depriving a little thing like you of a much-needed calorie or two.'

To her dismay Seven felt herself blushing as she shook her head. Even if she was famished she couldn't have taken a bite. It seemed too provocative, too . . . symbolic a gesture. A hard man like Jake Jackson was forbidden fruit to a girl like Seven.

Jake might have toyed with her embarrassment, but the little girl on the knoll suddenly took a tumble and burst into tears. Jake's entire body tensed and Seven waited for the mother to rush over and comfort her child. When there was no evidence of parental concern Jake leapt to his feet.

'Where in the hell is whoever's supposed to be looking after her?' he swore furiously.

Jake's long strides took him up the small hillock in seconds and Seven hurried to follow, afraid that his anger would transmit itself to the child and frighten rather than soothe her.

She needn't have worried. Watching Jake with the girl was a revelation. He crouched by her side, not touching her, just talking in a low voice. After a moment the girl uncovered her eyes and looked at him. From a distance Seven watched her smile uncertainly, her tears clearing up like magic as Jake continued to talk. His laugh, deep and entirely without the cynical edge which usually controlled it, was joined by a high-pitched giggle. When a concerned-looking young woman towing a baby in a pram arrived on the scene Jake was equally charming, banishing her obvious concern about a strange man accosting her child.

Their return to the library was swift and silent, but at the door Jake paused to sketch her a mocking bow.

'I'd like to say goodbye, but I have the distinct feeling that we'll be seeing each other again. Next time, maybe it'll be my turn to comfort you with apples...'

He left Seven searching her mind for the quotation and being oddly shocked when she located it. It was from the Bible, the Song of Solomon. 'Stay me with flagons, comfort me with apples: for I am sick of love.'

It was late-night closing for the library, and by the time Seven locked the doors just after eight o'clock she was fed up with herself for letting thoughts of Jake Jackson distract her to the point of carelessness during the rest of the long day.

Unfortunately, she discovered, she wasn't shot of him yet. When she pulled up in her driveway, she noted with a sinking heart the egotistical personalised 'J.J.' number-plate on the sleek, black Jaguar lined up at the kerb. In front of it was a police-car, the sound of its radio crackling through the half-open window.

The house was ablaze with light and Seven's key faltered in the lock. He could have had the decency to warn her this afternoon what she would be coming home to.

But then, obviously Jake Jackson didn't *have* any decency. He had got under her guard by acting like a sensitive human being and now that sensitive human being was having her aunt arrested!

Seven rushed inside. To her relief the embarrassing parlour was empty, but when she entered the small, neat but slightly shabby living-room she uttered a little squeak of disbelief at the sight that greeted her. There wasn't a handcuff or uniform in sight! Instead, Jake Jackson was leaning against the brick mantelpiece holding—Seven's shock soared—a glass of Aunt Jane's revoltingly sweet sherry. She gaped at him for a moment before looking at the brawny young man sitting on the couch with her aunt. He rose, smiling his recognition over the top of his glass, and Seven blushed.

'Seven—you're here at last! You remember Detective Hedges, don't you?' Her aunt beamed excitedly.

How could she forget her aunt's 'tame policeman'? He had once stolen a kiss and asked her to dinner, but she had shyly turned him down. Apart from the fact that she had known he was married, she hadn't been sure whether the brash young man was serious or not. How embarrassing it would have been if she had been tempted into ignoring her moral scruples only to find out that he had been teasing!

'Yes, of course. Hello, Detective,' she murmured awkwardly, and his hazel eyes twinkled.

'Duncan,' he reminded her boldly, taking her hand. 'I'm a Detective Inspector now...and divorced.'

Seven removed her hand and backed away, her flush deepening at the implication of that gratuitous piece of information. Her eyes collided nervously with Jake's and slid away. His indigo gaze was speculative as he looked from her embarrassed face to that of the amused detective. She imagined his grubby newsman's mind adding up the score and including a few extra sleazy zeros.

'Seven, guess what?' her aunt interrupted the silent by-play. 'Mr Hedges has found the house—you know, the house in the picture.'

'*What?*' It was the last thing she was expecting to hear.

'Yes. Isn't it wonderful? Of course, I had a rough idea of where it would be,' her aunt lied with blithe confidence, 'but I never guessed it would be so easy. After all, the picture is a representation of the way it would have looked six years ago. Fortunately Mr Hedges says that it hasn't changed much——'

'It was actually a bit of a coincidence——' Duncan Hedges began, but Aunt Jane wouldn't allow that.

'There's no such thing as coincidence, Mr Hedges...it's predetermination——'

A snort from the fireplace.

'Please, Aunt Jane, just let Mr—let Duncan tell the story,' said Seven hurriedly. Jake looked in the mood to ram his sherry glass down somebody's throat. She could see his incredulity straining at the leash and knew instinctively that he was hating this. Hating it with a passion. And yet he was here, enduring it. Why?

'I heard that your aunt had sent the drawing in, and I knew that the guy who originally handled the case had retired and that no one specific was assigned because of its file status...after a certain length of time a file can still be open but inactive.' Duncan tossed an apologetic look at Jake, who ignored him in favour of the grainy remains of his sherry. Evidently the two men hadn't hit it off. 'The detective whose desk the picture ended up on wasn't very interested so I asked if he minded me nosing around on my own. Of course, I had the advantage of knowing that Jane wasn't the joke he seemed to think she was. In fact I might not be a D.I. today if some of her hunches hadn't favourably graced my record...'

Maybe Duncan wasn't so much Aunt Jane's tame policeman as she was his tame psychic, thought Seven wryly. He had kept pretty quiet about the 'hunches' as they occurred, she recalled, and only after the event did he welcome the publicity—almost as much as Aunt Jane did. Yes...in discreetly sticking his neck out over the years he had certainly enhanced his chances of promotion.

'I couldn't believe it when I saw the sketch. You see, I'd visited the place only last week on a drug bust. It's a boarding house, has been for the last twenty years, and I doubt whether it's had a new lick of paint in all that time. The old guy who runs the place wasn't involved in the drug bust, but it's in a tough part of town and I wouldn't be surprised if he knew what was going on and just turned a blind eye for the sake of expediency. He drinks a bit, but not enough to loosen his tongue so I had to lean on him a bit. He remembered the Jackson case but he didn't recognise her photograph. He did, however, have a couple with a baby girl staying round about that time—which he specifically remembered because it was the first and last time he rented to anyone with kids or pets. The kid yowled all the time, he said, and the couple fought like cat and dog for the whole two weeks they were there. But he said the baby had black hair and was only eighteen months old.'

Oh, God, how could Jake bear this? Duncan had deliberately built the hope, only to demolish it. Without even being fully aware of her action Seven had gradually edged across the room, and now she took the empty glass that Jake was twirling back and forth in his hand, resisting the powerful urge to touch him.

'I...I'll get you another,' she said quietly, to make contact with his frigid remoteness.

'Now you're *encouraging* me to drink?' he remarked with stony irony. 'I don't need to be stayed with flagons, *yet*...I think I need to be stone-cold deadly sober to hear this, don't you? Getting drunk isn't going to make this sound any saner——'

'Jake——'

'Hang on, Seven, you haven't heard it yet,' Duncan called her attention back. 'The guy's wife remembers the baby, too, but she remembers from a woman's point of view. She said the mother was very possessive, wouldn't let the child out of her sight, or let anyone else touch her. But the wife got a good look one day and said there was something odd about her. She had very blue eyes and fair skin for a brunette, and she looked a lot more mature than eighteen months. So I went away and got the police artist to re-colour a picture of Rebecca, and both the wife and one of the other former residents I tracked down who had the rooms next door recognised her. It's amazing what a simple change of hair colour can achieve... especially in a child, because their features aren't as distinctive as an adult's.'

'Who were they—who were the couple?' asked Seven tersely.

'We don't know yet,' said Duncan regretfully. 'This guy's records are in a mess, although he's been audited in the last ten years so he's been keeping receipts, but they're all in boxes in his attic and there's no telling how accurate they really are. It's all pretty flimsy, too flimsy for the department to agree to assign a lot of manpower to, so I'll be working on this one alone, along with my other cases, of course. Mr Jackson has already put a private detective on the case working from another angle——'

Ah, the source of conflict. Duncan's voice told Seven he was not at all pleased at the thought of sharing the glory.

'I haven't *put* a man on the case. He's still on it. Unlike the police, he never shoved the file into the oblivion of "unsolved".'

Seven was surprised. Charlotte said that her son had given up hope, and yet he had continued to employ a detective?

'That's hardly fair, Mr Jackson,' Duncan pointed out. 'After all, the department doesn't have the unlimited resources that you apparently do. There are other crimes to be investigated which are just as important to their victims——'

'I'm sure he didn't mean to imply otherwise,' said Seven hurriedly, earning herself an unappreciative look from both men for her attempted peace-making 'I...what happens now?'

'What happens now is that we move in with Jake and Charlotte,' Jane Selkirk chirped cheerfully. 'I'm already packed. We were just waiting for you.'

'What?' Seven dropped the glass, which Jake neatly caught at knee-level. He tilted his head to smile grimly at her appalled expression.

'You and me both, mouse,' he said, too softly for the others to hear.

Duncan's square, handsome face was enthusiastic. 'Jane thinks that she'll have more success with her "prescient indicators" if she is steeped and surrounded by the strong memories of Rebecca that exist in her home...'

It was a prime example of Aunt Jane double-talk and Seven jerked her horrified gaze away from Jake, not wanting to see his justifiable contempt. Even she, a believer, privately derided the jargon that tried to explain the inexplicable.

'No. It's impossible. I can't leave the house...and my job——'

'Don't be silly, Seven.' Her aunt dismissed her feeble protests with a tinkling wave of her hand. 'You must come. You know you must, because I won't go and live in a strange house without you. If anything, the Jacksons' house is *closer* to the library than ours, so you don't have to worry about getting to your job. Mr Jackson has come here specially to make the offer on behalf of himself and his mother, and it's only common humanity to accept!'

Jake Jackson offering to let a psychic live openly in his home? There had to be an ulterior motive and Seven refused to support it.

'No.' She shook her head, putting her hands behind her back to hide their trembling, clenching her fists to help give her the courage to say, 'It's utterly, totally, *completely* out of the question. I'm sorry, but that's just the way it is!'

CHAPTER FIVE

'SO *YOU'RE* J.J.'s little country cousin!'

'I...I beg your pardon?' Seven's fingers tightened around her wine glass as she turned to face the tall dark woman who had come up behind her.

'The relation staying at J.J's place.' The silent word in the sentence—*poor*—was added before 'relation' by the flick of dark brown eyes over Seven's demure green wool dress. It was her best, but she knew it didn't match up in glamour terms with most of those at the party— particularly this woman in her silver and black sophistication.

'Actually I'm no relation at all, and I've lived all my life in the city,' Seven said stiffly. It wasn't the first time she had had to fend off the avid curiosity of professionals. It hadn't been her choice to accompany Jake and Charlotte to this Media Event—the presentation of annual journalism awards. But then, when in the last few days had she been allowed any choice about anything?

She would have been able to resist the appalling idea of moving in with the Jacksons if it had only been Aunt Jane she had been up against—after all, she had plenty of experience at vetoing her aunt's crazier schemes. She might even have been able to resist Duncan Hedges' combination of forthright logic and flattering persuasion, but Jake Jackson...well, it was apparent that no one had yet resisted him and survived to tell the tale! Instead of pooh-poohing the idea with his customary brutal scepticism he had put all his considerable muscle behind seeing it carried out. When Seven had protested that she didn't think that he wanted them in his house he had zeroed in on her with those devastating air-force blue eyes and let loose his arsenal. He had told her bluntly that he didn't give a damn what she thought. He wanted her and her crazy aunt where he could keep an eye on them. He told her that all he was interested in was getting results, and if that meant cohabiting with the devil himself he'd move into hell, so he certainly wasn't going to balk at stirring the pot with a couple of self-proclaimed and possibly self-deluded witches. He told her that what he *wanted* was for her to get her flat little behind into gear or he'd do it for her. Bludgeoned into acquiescence by the combined weight of their opinion, Seven had found herself meekly going away to pack, all the while cursing herself for her weakness.

His attitude had set the tone for a very uncomfortable stay. Aunt Jane had taken to their more luxurious surroundings like a duck to water, unaffected by Jake's surly suspicion and contempt, but Seven had found the situation more distressing with each passing day. She couldn't relax in his house, she was too sensitive to its tense atmosphere, to the conflicting forces at work there. She didn't see very much of Jake himself; his mother had understated the matter when she had told them that he worked long hours—Seven thought they were crippling—but even when he wasn't there she was aware of the force of his personality, lingering in the house like a haunting fragrance.

Haunted. That was what her aunt had said one night at dinner—the Jackson house was haunted by the unquiet spirit of Rebecca. It had been on the only occasion that Jake had dined with them and he had reacted to the statement with an internal violence that had frightened her. He had stood up and walked out without a word, leaving his meal hardly touched, but as he'd passed the back of her chair Seven had felt the hairs on the nape of her neck rise and her heart pulse heavily with shock. Not long afterwards she had had to excuse herself and only just made it to the bathroom in time. Her appetite since had been erratic, non-existent at breakfast and dinner and ravenous at lunchtime. The peculiar way that Cilla eyed her as she wolfed down enormous lunches made her wonder whether the girl thought her bulimic. Seven wouldn't blame her. For despite the amount of food she gorged every lunchtime she had lost several pounds that she could ill afford to lose.

'Really?' She was still under the microscope and she moved uneasily as she suddenly recognised the woman. Hadn't she won an award for investigative journalism? And wasn't she employed by Jake's major opposition? 'So you're just friends, then?'

Seven almost smiled at the irony. How would the woman react if she said sweetly that they were quite the opposite? But Seven knew better than to throw a mad dog a bone. 'You might say that,' she said non-committally.

'*Good* friends? I suppose you must be, since I've never known J.J. to take his girlfriends home to live with his mother before.'

'Uh...have you known him long?' Seven asked evasively.

The carmine mouth curved. She really was breathtakingly lovely, Seven decided dispassionately, if you ignored the hard glint in the dark eyes. 'Long and intimately,' the woman said. 'That's why I quit his paper. If you sleep with the boss you risk your professional reputation.'

'Oh,' said Seven faintly, taking a hurried sip of her wine. These journalists seemed to enjoy trying to outshock each other with their gossip and back-biting, and she was no match for their candour.

'Oh, don't worry,' said the other woman, enjoying Seven's discomfort. 'It's over now. But I should warn you that J.J. isn't known for his staying power. Where did you say you came from?'

'I don't think I did.' Seven finished her glass and looked around. Maybe she could excuse herself to go and find another drink, although she had had more than enough. Her head was beginning to ache.

'Someone said you're a librarian. Was that just a joke or is it true?' Her voice expressed the doubt that Jake could ever be interested in a woman who did something so commonplace for a living, and Seven felt like snapping back, telling her what the *real* joke was, but she sensed that that was just what the woman wanted.

'It's true.'

'No kidding?' A little laugh. 'So you share a love of literature as well, huh?'

As well as what? Seven didn't dare ask. 'I would hardly call the *Clarion* literature,' she said tightly, and the waiting predator pounced.

'Oh, what would you call it?'

'I really think I should be——' Seven began edging away.

'Are you sleeping together?'

She didn't ask it quietly and Seven went scarlet as a little silence fell nearby.

Across the room Charlotte Jackson frowned. 'Oh, dear...'

'What's the matter, aren't you feeling well?' Her son half turned protectively towards her.

'I am, but I don't think that Seven is. I really shouldn't have drifted away like that. She told me she's not used to crushes like this——'

'For goodness' sake, Mother, she may not look like it but she's a grown woman. I'm sure she can cope——'

'No, you're not. You just don't care. You were the one who insisted she come along tonight—you could have at least introduced her round instead of throwing her to the wolves.'

'Don't you mean the wolverines?' murmured Jake, having found the subject of their conversation with a quick look that betrayed his foreknowledge. She was looking small and hunted, the cynosure of a circle of eyes. Even at this distance he could see that she was flustered. He'd never known a woman who blushed so readily. It irritated the hell out of him—made him want to tell her not to be such an easy target.

'It's that awful Tracey woman,' his mother was saying anxiously. 'She tried to pump me earlier, you know, Jake, about Seven, but I stuck to our story. I'd better go and see what's going on——'

'No, you stay here,' he growled. 'Steven'll be back with your drink in a minute. I'll go.'

'Jake.' His mother stayed him with a maternal tug on his evening jacket. 'Don't be——' She faltered under his cool stare. 'You don't treat her very well, you know...'

'Did you expect me to?' he asked tightly.

'If you blame anyone it should be me, or Jane. Poor Seven is just the meat in the sandwich. It's not her fault that her aunt is succeeding where y...everyone else failed. And she is, isn't she, Jake?' his mother said quietly. 'You scoffed at first, but you can't deny it, even if you won't admit it out loud——'

'This isn't the time or the place.' He shrugged off her restraining hand and pushed through the crowd, ignoring the calls on his attention. As he got within earshot and heard the question that Tina Tracey was reiterating his anger increased. Maybe dragging Seven Selkirk along tonight hadn't been such a good idea after all. It might have been a good demonstration of control, but it also presented her with the perfect opportunity for revenge. If she spilled the beans here—and Tina was an expert with a tin-opener—all his clever manoeuvring would be wasted.

'Found out anything worth printing, Tina?' he asked smoothly as he insinuated himself between the two women, his arm sliding around Seven's narrow waist. He felt her stiffen and his fingers curved warningly into her taut flesh.

Tina was unembarrassed. She grinned at him; she had built her considerable reputation on her brashness. 'Are you kidding? Secretive, isn't she? I might have known she wasn't the push-over she looks. You never did like the kiss-and-tell type, except in the line of business. I doubt I could get anything out of your mystery woman with a crowbar. She's very good at very pleasantly saying nothing. Not a diplomat is she...or a diplomat's wife...?'

Jake ignored the sly suggestion, which, in view of Seven's lack of rings, was an obvious ploy to provoke a reaction. Instead he glanced down at the woman tucked against the angle of his body. Secretive? Mystery woman? Little Miss Mouse who revealed every thought in her face with the transparency of a child? Had Tina's sharp instincts about people slipped up for once? At that moment Seven looked up and he received a small, unpleasant shock. Maybe it was his instinct which had been faulty. She was still blushing, but her winter-grey eyes were as obscure as smoked glass, as if she had distanced herself from what was happening around her, retreating to a place of safety within herself. He probed for some indication of her thoughts and came up blank. If it was only shyness that made her draw back into her fragile shell, how come Tina hadn't winkled some innocent answers out of her? If she *was* so innocent. The private detective's report had been fairly comprehensive but it was all hearsay. There was plenty about what other people thought and felt and said about Seven Selkirk but nothing from *her*. Jane Selkirk, to his intense irritation, never *stopped* talking. In a few short days she had driven him mad with her noise. But her niece was the opposite. She fitted herself neatly into her aunt's shadow, drifting around like a small cloud, quiet and remote in an almost cloudless sky, keeping high up out of everyone's notice. But even small, unnoticed clouds could bring storms. She responded when she was spoken to, he had noticed, but never initiated any conversation, even though he knew from her qualifications that she was intelligent. Come to think of it, it was almost as if she was *afraid* of talking. Her aunt was undoubtedly a compulsive liar, even to the extent that she believed her own lies, which made them almost impossible to sort out. But Seven was the conscientious type. She knew the difference between right and wrong, truth and lies. So what was her caution concealing? It suddenly became imperative to find out—*now*.

'Any announcement about Seven and me will be issued at the appropriate time,' he said slickly, diverting their listeners as he whisked the astounded woman at his side away. 'Now, if you don't mind, I have someone I want Seven to meet...'

'What on earth did you say that for?' Seven whispered anxiously as she stumbled to keep up with him. 'Do you know what you just did?'

'Yes, I just saved your precious reputation,' he stated tersely, and unfairly, she thought, since he was the one who had jeopardised it in the first place by insisting on the public 'cover story' of friendship for her and her aunt's presence in his house.

'You implied—you said...now everyone thinks that you and I are...are having an affair.'

'They thought that anyway. Your blushes were a dead give-away. This way at least we give the affair the semblance of respectability.' He turned a corner and went down a couple of flights of stairs and through another door and they were in one of the hotel bars. Considering the celebrating going on upstairs, the bar was doing a lethally quiet trade. Jake thrust her on to a high stool at one end of the bar and signalled the somnambulant barman.

'A whisky on the rocks and a medium white wine for the lady.'

'I don't want anything else to drink,' said Seven, squirming to try to get her feet to the floor.

Jake stilled her with a heavy hand on her thigh. 'Humour me,' he said, in a very unamused voice.

Her mouth tucked into a stubborn straight line. 'Soda water, then please.'

'Make it a spritzer,' Jake modified as the barman turned to comply.

Seven opened her mouth to object and then snapped it closed as Jake leant on the bar, inclining his head down towards her. Surely he wasn't going to...? He kept coming as she tilted further and further back on the stool, her eyes almost crossing with the effort of keeping the proper distance between his mouth and hers. 'All right, a spritzer would be fine. Lovely,' she said breathlessly, and almost fainted with relief when he stopped his silent onslaught 'I'm really quite thirsty,' she continued, with an unconvincing little laugh. 'Thank you,' she added with polite desperation, as her back ached with the strain of holding the off-balance pose.

His eyes were black in the dimness of the muted bar lighting as he slowly drew back, releasing her from the bondage of his nearness. She began to breathe again until he said suddenly, 'You have a very sexy mouth.'

The mouth in question fell open.

'And you have breasts.' His tone was almost one of accusation.

Seven swept a frantic look at the barman's back. 'Of course I do—I'm a woman, aren't I?'

'I had my doubts. All those pin-tucks and frills you wear, I thought it was to hide the fact you're as flat as a board. But in that dress you look positively lush.'

Seven automatically splayed a protective hand across her thinly covered chest. It was true that the dress was much more simply cut than her usual attire; it hugged her form instead of draping it. But he had no right to make her sound like a...a brazen hussy for possessing the usual female equipment!

'Unless it's all padding,' he added, outrageously, needling her.

'I wish it were!' slipped out wrathfully as the barman came back with their drinks. Given the slenderness of her frame, she had always felt self-consciously top-heavy.

Jake paid for the drinks without looking at the denomination of the note he handed across the bar. His eyes narrowed thoughtfully as he watched her squirm when she realised what her exclamation had told him.

'Is that why you wear those long-line jackets and pouchy blouses all the time?' he guessed accurately. To hide an *over*-endowment? What an odd woman you are. I would have thought you'd be keen to flaunt it. Full breasts, slender waist and hips...what more could a woman want?'

'From a man's point of view, probably nothing,' returned Seven, flattered in spite of herself. She set her mouth in the prim line she knew annoyed him. 'I'd rather be judged on my intelligence, thank you. I don't like being *leered* at. I'm not one of your...your page-three pin-ups!'

'Front page.'

'What?'

'We put them on the front page these days.'

'You would,' she said sourly, taking a drink out of her glass, holding it carefully up in front of her. His eyes glinted and she began to panic. As if she weren't aware enough of Jake Jackson as a man, he was now making her super-aware of her own femininity. And she didn't like it! The conversation was getting far too personal.

'What did you want me for, anyway?' In view of the conversation they had just had that sounded suggestive. 'I mean, why did you want to leave the party—tired of all the accolades?' To her surprise the *Clarion* had won a number of awards, from Best News Photograph to Best Front Page—one on which a pin-up had been mercifully missing!

Her slightly acid tone gave her away. 'I noticed you didn't rush to congratulate me. Were you annoyed to discover that I'm not the unmitigated trash-monger that you thought I was, Seven?' he mocked. 'Most people have hidden merits, if you care to look for them, why should I and mine be the exception?' His eyes dipped and she knew he was mocking her about her own hidden merits. Well, she wasn't going to conduct a conversation in innuendoes.

'Congratulations,' she said grudgingly. 'Although I don't happen to think that a few awards vindicates your style of journalism.'

His mouth twisted. 'You couldn't resist the rider, could you? Tell me, Seven, is there anything in this modern world of which you do approve without reservation?'

'Of course, there are a lot of things,' she protested, rejecting his image of her as a tireless fault-finder. 'I just happen to believe in some of the old-fashioned virtues, that's all. Like hard work and fair play and modesty and...and...'

'Honesty?'

Seven bit her lip and looked away. 'Yes,' she said guiltily.

'Well, *I'm* hard-working. I bought the *Clarion* when it was sick unto death and in five years I've worked my guts out to turn it around into a vibrant thriving award-winner with more advertising than we can comfortably cope with.'

Five years. So he had bought the paper after the tragedy. Made it his life and poured all his considerable energies into it. No wonder it had been a sensational success.

'As for fair play, I've always campaigned on the side of the underdog, against crime, big business crushing the little guy, the inarticulate, the voiceless——'

'It's not so much the content as the *style*,' Seven was forced to admit. 'I mean, you make everything so dramatic. You stir up trouble just for the sake of it——'

'Debate is always healthy, and what's life without a bit of drama and excitement?'

'I would have thought you'd had enough of that in your own life, not to go out seeking it in others——' Seven stopped, ashamed of herself for using such a tactic just to stop him winning a point.

'On the contrary,' he said quietly. 'What I went through engendered in me a rage against injustice that will always be with me. And the paper was a way of using that rage constructively. If I hadn't had it, I would have gone mad...and now, well—I'm hooked on the pressure and the pace.'

'I'm sorry...' Her voice was soft with remorse. 'I didn't mean to——'

'No, of course you didn't.' He accepted her apology with typical speed, turning it to his advantage. 'I should be flattered—after all, it's not often that you speak without stopping to think, is it? I find it very enlightening to discover that you have a vicious streak in you somewhere. Makes you less of a little paragon.'

'I never said I was perfect——'

'No, you just act as if you are. You know, one of the most valuable instincts I've developed over the years is the one that tells me there's more to a story than the facts would suggest. It's a kind of leap of the logical imagination that a lot of reporters don't have. They can still be good, but they'll never be great no matter how well they write. And my instincts about you, Seven

Selkirk, are giving me hell. Are you waiting for the pro-
pitious moments to tell me that you have my daughter
and for a certain consideration you'll hand her over?'

'No!' Seven rose, shaking with shocked outrage. She
had known he was suspicious, but the depth of that suspicion was frightening.

'Sit.' It was terse command and explicit threat all in
one. Seven subsided unsteadily.

'You can't think——'

'Why not? What else am I supposed to think? I've
done some research on the subject and there's no doubt
in my mind that if—and it's a very big if—there is such
a thing as true psychic ability, your aunt is the last type
of person to possess it. I've seen her in action over the
past few days and all she does is go through the
motions—she's all sound and fury and no substance.
Even her imagination is second-hand, a mish-mash of
incoherent ideas picked up from books and bad horror
movies. She has no originality, or sensitivity, she's im-
pervious to other people's opinions, let alone to their
thoughts or their so-called "auras". Therefore it follows
that the evidence of that "psychic drawing" was fab-
ricated, but equally obviously, judging by the results, it
had to have been based in fact. Somehow your aunt
picked up a morsel of information, probably through
that network of spiritualist weirdos and shady hangers-
on that she mixes with, and she decided to use it to
support her own delusions. Maybe you were part of that
and maybe you weren't. How about an amnesty? You
tell me what you know and I promise not to use it against
you or your aunt. But this is your last chance to come
clean, Seven. After this there'll be no quarter——'

'You sound like a bad detective novel——'

'Stop trying to change the subject. Do you expect your
aunt to come up with anything else?'

'Duncan Hedges thinks she will——'

'That's not an answer,' Jake pointed out harshly. He was all journalist now. No mockery, no humour leavened his hard, predatory curiosity. 'If I want to know what your friendly, neighbourhood divorcee thinks I'll ask him. I want to hear your honest opinion for once.'

Seven lifted her head bravely. 'If you're asking whether Aunt Jane or I know more about Rebecca than we're telling you, the answer is no, and I can tell you that Aunt Jane didn't get that drawing from any outsider.' She spoke quickly, hoping he wouldn't pick up that little betraying piece of truth. 'If Aunt Jane says that Rebecca is still alive, then you can believe her——'

'You really do believe that,' he realised with a savage, raking disappointment. 'How can you put your faith in something so bizarrely senseless?'

'It's better than not having faith in anything at all,' said Seven quietly.

He tossed back his whisky without enjoyment and ordered another with a brief glance at the half-full glass Seven was still nursing. 'I have faith in myself, that's all I need. It's brought me wealth and power—virtually everything I could want——'

'Except peace.'

There was a brief torment in the darkened eyes. 'Peace doesn't make good headlines. Haven't you heard the axiom: bad news is good news and good news is bad news? It's a newspaperman's creed.'

The truth sprang at her out of that fleeting torment. 'Why don't you want Rebecca found alive?' she asked with deep compassion.

For a moment she was afraid. He reared up. The strong, blunt knuckles went white around the glass as he fought to bring his white-hot flare of murderous rage under control. Then he looked at her, and his eyes were as cold as death. Until this moment he had not even been aware of the powerful suppressive instincts at work in his mind. He closed his eyes.

'Because I'm afraid.'

Seven, who had thought this tough, cynical man could brave anything, felt her chest constrict at the bald admission, and to her, of all people. 'Of what?'

His eyes opened, glittering with self-disgust. 'Of finding out that she hates me. That she suffered because of me. That it might have been better for her if she *had* died back then. I was her father but I wasn't there for her when she most needed a father's protection. My love failed her miserably. Oh, there's a whole list of reasons, all exquisitely selfish. I killed her, you see. In my mind I made her die, so that life would be a little easier for me. And if she's still alive, that was an unspeakable thing to do... She was only a baby. She probably doesn't remember me at all. Why should she? Why should she want to come back to a father who can't promise to keep her safe? Your aunt isn't the only fraud in my house.' It was a weak strike, his voice too raw and wounded to make the thrust telling.

'But you never stopped looking. Jake—you can't blame yourself for what happened. And for six years...six long years, even though you thought she was dead you kept on that detective—it must have cost you thousands over the years——'

'Blood money. A sop to my conscience. A quest of revenge, not of hope. I never really expected the detective to find anything—and he obliged. Who knows, if I had been more vigorous in demanding results I might have given him the incentive to put a greater effort into his job?' The second whisky slid down even more quickly than the first, but afforded no solace. 'Oh, you're right, little Miss Mouse, to despise me. I even capitalised on the notoriety her disappearance afforded by using people's curiosity about me to sell my papers. Before Rebecca was abducted I was just a damned good reporter working for someone else, afterwards I was a famous one, able to raise the extra money I needed to buy into the *Clarion* because the people I borrowed it from gave me compassionate terms. I traded on their guilt——'

'Jake, don't.' She reached out and placed a gentle hand on his arm, trying to stanch the flow of blistering self-contempt.

He cupped his hand over hers, measuring his strength against the movement of her pale, delicate fingers. 'You shouldn't ask unpleasant questions if you don't want to hear unpleasant answers. You know, you'd make a hell of a good journalist if you weren't so damned self-effacing. You've got more damaging admissions out of me tonight than any seasoned professional has ever been able to extract. And to think I dragged you down here so that I could get something out of *you*. Any other guilty secrets you want me to reveal while I'm on a roll?'

It was said with weary sarcasm, but there *was* a question which she had been dying to ask someone, and here, in the spurious intimacy of the empty bar she dared to do it.

'You . . . you said you don't have a wife, and no one ever mentions your marriage. I . . .' She swallowed at the lack of expression in his face and soldiered on. 'I just wondered when you got divorced . . . or is Rebecca's mother dead?'

'An interesting set of assumptions,' he murmured, adding, with some of his former mockery, 'I don't have a wife because I've never been married.'

'Oh!' Seven blushed. She realised her hand was still clasped beneath his, curving over the powerful contours of his warm forearm, and tried to tug it away. His fingers tightened.

'Rebecca's mother, Chloe, was my mistress.'

'It's really none of my business,' muttered Seven feverishly. The way his gravelly voice wrapped around the word 'mistress' made it sound even more sinful than it was. Her stool wobbled and she stopped her tugging, resigned to temporary captivity.

'I use the word "mistress" rather than "lover" because although we lived together it certainly wasn't an equal relationship,' he told her, adjusting his position against the bar so he could see her face better. 'At the time that was the way we both wanted it. Chloe called herself a model but she didn't work much. I was well paid and I had a private income from an inheritance so I didn't object to supporting her while I enjoyed the privilege of her exclusive favours. She was a beautiful woman, a little spoiled and lazy, but that's acceptable in a mistress. I didn't love her and she didn't love me so it was an ideal arrangement, but somewhere along the line Chloe decided that it wasn't enough. She wanted to be married. Her friends were all getting married and she thought we should, too. I made it very clear that it wasn't on the cards. I was ambitious, and to satisfy that ambition I couldn't afford to be tied down. I certainly wasn't going to get married just for the sake of it, just so that she could boast to her friends.

'Chloe pouted a bit but she dropped the subject, and I naturally assumed that since she stayed on my terms she had decided it wasn't important after all. I should have known better. Chloe didn't like to be thwarted. She stopped taking the Pill and got pregnant. She told my mother about it before she broke the news to me. She was quite pleased with her cleverness, quite open about the fact it had been deliberate. She didn't really want a baby, but if it was the only way to get a commitment out of me she thought it was worth a try. She was so casual about it I thought she was kidding at first. But she wasn't. She knew how keen my mother was on the idea of grandchildren and she knew I had a well-developed sense of responsibility. She was gambling on the combination of the two to work in her favour...' His mouth curved in very un-fond remembrance.

'But it didn't.' Seven was fascinated and appalled by this insight into his murky past. 'What did you do?'

'I gave her a commitment all right—just not the one she expected. I offered to support her through the pregnancy and accept my share of the responsibility for the baby afterwards. But that was it. No ring. Chloe being Chloe, she refused to believe me. She had it fixed in her mind that I was only dragging my heels, even when I made her move out and set her up in her own apartment. Right up until Rebecca's birth she was blithely certain that I'd give in and marry her for the sake of legitimising my child. Afterwards she couldn't avoid inconvenient reality. She was stuck on her own with a very demanding infant to care for. Not Chloe's thing at all. So after a few months she finally gave up.'

'Gave up?' Seven sensed what was coming, but still found it hard to believe.

'Cut her losses. Walked out—minus encumbrances. Left Rebecca with my mother one morning and didn't come back to pick her up. Eight months later she posted me a wedding photo. She married some property entrepreneur in Hawaii—much more Chloe's speed.'

'And Rebecca? I mean, did she come back and see her?'

He shrugged. 'Once she was gone I didn't expect her to. Becky was never anything more to her than a means to an end. Chloe didn't have a lot of emotional depth—that's why she was such a good mistress. She was absolutely determined that she was going to have the baby, but I don't think she thought of it as real. The irony is that my refusal to bow to her blackmail tied me up far more securely than a bad marriage ever would have. Suddenly there was this tiny, dependent human being in my life. My mother was happy to look after her while I worked, but made certain that I was responsible the rest of the time. It was very clever of her... her way of making sure that I acknowledged the bond, and that

Becky wouldn't suffer for not having a mother. And it worked. Rather better than even my mother expected it to. Suddenly writing about other people's problems and traumas wasn't the supreme challenge in my life—getting that little baby to stop crying and smile for me was. I discovered the incredible rewards and frustrations of close parenting. I was the one who got up for night feeds, walked the floor when she teethed, agonised over her growth patterns, carried baby pictures around in my wallet and was generally insufferably smug about how perfect she was. I rebuilt my life around her. I bought that house for the three of us, near to a good school, I stopped taking overseas assignments, I cut down on the booze and partying—occupational hazards for single journalists—and generally became a mellower, much more likeable human being in the process...'

Until his rebuilt world had been destroyed overnight. Rebecca had taught her father how to love, and the bleeding vacuum that had been created when that love had been abruptly torn away had been refilled with a bitter determination not to be hurt that way again. Through his work he had exhibited a brutal callousness that in fact masked a vulnerability far greater even than Seven's.

'When Becky disappeared, you don't think Chloe——?'

'Had anything to do with it? No—not her style. Chloe is a bit greedy but not vindictive, although the police naturally checked her out. She sent me a sympathy card.'

'Oh, Jake——'

'That phrase seems to be a current favourite of yours.' He smiled crookedly at her small face, at the misty grey eyes that were rain-washed with sweet, aching sorrow. 'You're not going to waste tears on a hard case like me, are you? I can look after myself. You I have doubts about. Under the shy, spiky exterior beats the heart of pure sucker. How do you know I haven't just been playing on your emotions in order to get under your guard?' And then he ruined it by touching her face gently and murmuring broodingly, 'When you look at me like that you remind me of Becky, full of the unexplored mysteries of life, full of trust that I would never do anything to hurt her. And look what happened. I'm not to be trusted, Seven, remember that. Hold on to your prim disapproval of crude profiteer of human misery that I am. If you don't I'll hurt you. I want to, you know,' he told her cruelly. 'I want to wipe that look of innocence away, to pick your secrets to pieces so that you lose the power of their protection. Stay away from me, Seven; don't make me punish you for someone else's sins . . .'

CHAPTER SIX

SEVEN'S eyes rounded in shocked fascination as she turned the page. Did people actually *do* those kinds of things to each other——?

There was a sound in the doorway and she jumped. When she saw the man shrugging out of his jacket she quickly stuffed the tabloid behind her, down between the cushions of the couch. She leaned forward to pick up the discarded book on the coffee-table, and by the time Jake looked up from loosening his tie and undoing the top button of his shirt she was demurely absorbed in a history of the early settlement of New Zealand.

'Where is everyone?' Jake growled, as he slung his jacket over the back of a chair and ran a hand through his slightly damp hair.

Not in the best of moods, obviously. 'Aunt Jane and your mother went out. Is it still raining?'

'Mmm...it's filthy out there.' He frowned. 'Where did they go?'

'To the movies.' In spite of the great disparity of their backgrounds and interests, Aunt Jane and Charlotte had become rather firmer friends than either Seven or Jake would have liked.

'Oh? What did they go and see?'

Seven hesitated. *'Ghostbusters,'* she admitted reluctantly, braced for a typical onslaught of scorn. To her surprise Jake laughed. He dropped into the chair opposite, still laughing, and she was disconcerted by his evident good humour, after the scowl he had worn when he entered.

'It was your mother's idea,' she told him firmly. 'Aunt Jane just happened to see the advertisement for it in this morning's paper, and Charlotte said that she hadn't seen it when it first came out.'

'Whereas, of course, your aunt had.'

At least a dozen times, but Seven wasn't about to hand him that piece of ammunition. 'It's a very funny film.'

'I know. I'm sure Mother will enjoy it.'

Seven was flabbergasted. 'Are you feeling all right?' she asked.

'A bit tired. I had a tense day. Why?'

'Oh, no reason,' she said hastily.

'Am I such a bad-tempered brute that you think that I must be delirious if I crack a smile?' he asked with a mocking lift of an eyebrow.

'Yes,' she said flatly. 'Particularly if it's got anything to do with Aunt Jane. You can barely be civil to her, let alone find anything she does amusing.'

'Maybe she's converting me into a believer...or do I mean subverting?'

That little bite was more like the Jake Jackson she knew. 'I doubt it. You're too opinionated. The only person you'll allow to convert you is yourself.'

'You know me so well,' he drawled, but didn't take the bait. 'What are you reading?'

She thought of the newspaper she had thrust behind her and blushed. 'A history of pre-European settlement in New Zealand.'

His head was tilted against the back of his chair, the navy eyes surveying her thought half-closed lids. 'Really? Such a mundane subject to put you to blush...or are you just reading the spicy bits?'

Seven shifted in embarrassment, and to her horror a distinct crackle came from the cushions beneath her. She froze.

Newspaperman that he was, Jake identified the sound immediately. His lids lifted, along with his brows. 'Are you sitting on something?'

'N-no, I don't think so,' Seven denied quickly, too quickly, clutching her open book to her chest.

Jake leant forward and, thinking he was about to get up and call her bluff, Seven quickly discovered innocently, 'Oh, yes, so I am.' She retrieved the *Clarion* and refolded it neatly. She almost murmured, 'I wonder how that got there?' but one look at Jake's face deterred her. He was wearing a smug, knowing smile that neatly framed her guilt.

'Been doing some literary slumming, have we, Miss Selkirk?'

The chill in her grey eyes couldn't counterbalance the hot flush in her cheeks. 'I was just reading the editorial!' she lied loftily, not having got that far yet.

'Mmm, you mean you didn't linger over the line-up of bare—er—cheeked male life-savers on page eight?' he asked wickedly, and was rewarded with an even greater ice/flame contrast. She threw the paper at him and he fielded it with a grin. 'You might well blush! You'll be shocked to know that people like you make up a big proportion of our sales. The illicit readers who sneak them into their supermarket trolleys so they don't have to suffer the intellectual humiliation of actually *asking* for such trash at the counter.'

'I didn't buy it. I just looked at it because it was here,' said Seven haughtily. Jake had all the major daily newspapers delivered to his house. 'I told you, I don't usually read the papers.'

'But you made an exception for mine. I'm flattered.'

'Don't be. It's really unexceptional. I won't bother picking it up again. How can you settle for producing something like that when you could do so much better?'

'You sound like my teachers—it was always: ''John has ability but could do better.'' But better in what way?

They meant I could score higher points by conforming, by sticking to the tried and true instead of trail-blazing on my own. Well, that was never my way and it never will be. I like to experiment; I like to prove that my way is just as damned good, if not better than other people's. I suppose you got glowing reports from your schools...'

'I didn't go to school until I was nearly thirteen.'

'You mean you did correspondence lessons until then?'

Jake settled back in his chair and Seven was so relieved that he wasn't going to pursue her embarrassment that she said frankly, 'I mean we travelled so much with the circus that the truant officers never seemed to catch up with us. But that doesn't mean we didn't learn anything,' she said, when she thought she saw silent criticism of her parents in his eyes. 'Quite the reverse. There were people from all sorts of backgrounds who joined us from time to time, and circus people are great natural teachers—they love to pass on their knowledge. Morgan and I learned Italian and French from the time we were babies, and mid-European history from people who had actually *experienced* some of it. We learned maths by helping sell tickets and count the takings, and reading and writing by helping to make posters and publicity flyers and programmes. My mother didn't have much formal education herself, but she knew the value of it, she just kept putting off the awful moment that she would have to send us away to school, and Morgan and I, well...' a wry smile '... we didn't like the idea much, either. Dad said we were too smart for school. He had a good education but never bothered to use it. He didn't think children should be cooped up and force-fed information, he thought life was the best teacher, and he thought the circus offered the best life of all. After all, it had given him all that he needed, including a wife— my mother was a tumbler in another circus when they met...' Her voice dropped to a whisper as she said, 'We had dozens of albums of photos and cuttings, but I don't even have a picture of them, or us all together...they were destroyed in the fire...'

'The one that killed your parents?'

Her face shuttered. 'Yes. That was when Morgan and I went to live with Aunt Jane, and started our proper schooling. We both had to struggle at first, and Morgan never really adjusted, but when I got used to the routine I loved school. I liked having all that knowledge and information available for the asking—having a real library with thousands of books, not just the few we could carry around with us.'

He had read the Press files. He knew that she and her sister had been staying in a neighbouring caravan on the night of the fire, which the coroner had decided was caused by a gas leak, sparked by a heater. But there was more than sadness and regret in her closed expression...much more. He was too shrewd, too experienced in the extraction of information to make the mistake of pressing her when it was obvious that she was already regretting her openness, so for the second time that evening he ignored an opening and allowed her to think she had succeeded in diverting him entirely.

'Do you miss it...the life you had then?'

'No.' She was unaware of the slight wistfulness of her expression. 'It's not the kind of thing I'd want to do with my adult life. Naturally I missed the family closeness we had—everyone's kin in the circus—but I think we were lucky to leave before the shine wore off. As children Morgan and I thought it all very glamorous and exciting, but it's a lot of hard work and worry running that kind of small operation. You have to be a certain type of person to devote your life to it, and I'm not that type.'

'What about your sister?'

'Morgan never seems to stay long enough in one place to become a type,' said Seven with a smile at the thought of the last hurried postcard she had received from the Middle East.

'I'm surprised your aunt hasn't run away to join the circus. She *does* seem the type.'

'Not really. Aunt Jane likes her creature comforts. Besides, to her it's not a way of life, it's just a——' She stopped, suddenly remembering to whom she was speaking.

'Game?'

'I——' He didn't look angry but she had discovered that Jake was adept at misleading expressions. It gave him fertile ground on which to spring his unexpected questions. She looked down at her lap and caught sight of her watch. 'Goodness, is that the time?'

'Yes, nine o'clock, far too early for you to start making noises about going to bed—alone, anyway. Has Mrs Taylor left any dinner for me?'

Seven was thrown by that little suggestive comment 'Er—no. She didn't make anything. Aunt Jane and Charlotte went to a café before the movie, and you said you had a big business lunch——'

'It was cancelled. We had a problem with the presses and it was panic stations for most of the afternoon. God, what a terrible day, and now I'm famished to boot. What did you have to eat?'

'I . . . I wasn't very hungry.' As usual the house had had a depressive effect on her appetite, even though she had skimped on lunch because Cilla had been off sick and they had been short-handed.

'You never are. No wonder you look so breakable—what you eat wouldn't keep a mouse alive. Come into the kitchen and I'll whip up something.'

He rose wearily, making her aware of the tiredness in and around his penetrating eyes and the slackness around his normally cynically tight mouth. Jake burned furious amounts of energy to sustain the hectic pace of his life. Sometimes she felt exhausted just watching him whirl in and out of the house. Every problem was a crisis, and every crisis was there to be solved...by him. And the fuel that he converted to energy was opposition. It exhilarated him, which was why he made such a dangerous enemy both inside and outside his newspaper.

'Why don't you let me do it?' she heard herself offer. 'You just relax and have a drink and I'll see what's in the fridge.'

There was not a man alive who could have refused such a feminine gesture of submission. But then Jake wasn't a man who conformed to expectations. 'No, thanks, you'd probably just offer me a wedge of cheese. Come on, stop looking a gift horse in the mouth. You can be *sous-chef* if you can't bear to stand idle...on the condition that you eat with me.'

'Oh, but I'm not——'

'Hungry? Yes, you are...you just don't realise it yet. Wait until you see the temptations I can offer you...'

She didn't have to wait to see *that*, thought Seven wryly as she watched him move around the narrow galley-kitchen. With his shirt half unbuttoned and his sleeves rolled up above his elbows he was a far more tempting display of masculinity than that team of self-consciously virile young Adonises who had posed for the *Clarion* with naked rears after the drunken end to a surf life-saving carnival in Australia. She had been able to admire them in a strictly detached, physical way. Jake's appeal was more earthy—unique, imperfect, unpredictable. Depending on his mood he could send a jolt of anger or pure pleasure to her bones. Now, as he bustled domestically around the kitchen, managing to look far more at home there than even Mrs Taylor did, Seven found herself perilously close to affectionate amusement. How did the horrible man do it?

'I didn't know that you knew how to cook,' she said, watching as he did clever things with a cleaver and a frozen piece of rump steak, shaving paper-thin slices off it and slinging them into a glutinous marinade.

'But then you don't know much about me at all, do you, Seven, except what your own prejudices tell you? Chloe hated cooking so I learned while we were living together. I find it very relaxing, very undemanding after a day like today. Would you wash those vegetables for me, please?'

'I don't recognise you when you're polite,' she was unable to resist saying drily as she dealt with the cabbage and celery and carrots and placed them on his chopping board.

'Charm doesn't achieve as much as rudeness in my business. Provocation is the name of the game.'

'Don't you get tired of it—the constant furore?'

'Don't you get tired of all that deadly quietness and numbing routine in your job?'

'It's not deadly and every job has its dull routines,' she told him hotly. 'But I'm never bored because each day is different, and there are always new books and new ideas to discover. People have very odd ideas about libraries. We're not archaic backwaters, you know. A suburban library, especially one our size, is a kind of community centre and meeting place—we get all sorts of interesting people coming in. I love my job and I'm proud of what I do!'

He paused in his chopping. 'My sentiments exactly!'

'How can you have pride in——?' She stopped as he turned the knife speculatively in his hand.

'Now who's being rude?' he said with a grin at her unease, calmly beginning to chop again. 'I suppose you don't stock copies of my disgusting rag in your sub-urban storehouse of knowledge?'

'That's the buyer's responsibility at Main Branch,' said Seven stiffly, knowing he had her there. 'But as it happens I don't believe in rigid censorship. We have lots of books on our shelves that I think don't deserve the space, but that's only my personal opinion. I wouldn't seek to impose it on everyone else.'

'You surprise me, mouse, I thought that's exactly what you were trying to do with your snide remarks about the *Clarion*. In fact you're in fairly dubious company. There are a lot of shady, and so-called upright, characters who would agree with you. They'd be delighted if public prudery and censorship laws prevented their lies and dirty business and personal practices from reaching the ears and eyes of their victims.'

'I just think you could do it with a little more...taste, that's all,' said Seven stubbornly.

He gave a shout of laughter as he tipped the meat slices into a seasoned wok heating on the gas element and began to stir-fry with gusto.

'Taste? Seven, that's an alien word to some of the people who appear in our pages. Their actions are tasteless in the extreme and there's no way on this earth to dress them up in pretty clothes. Tasteless, raw and real...that's the way many people live these days. I'm not saying its a good thing, only that it *is so*, and no amount of protest is going to change reality. Speaking of taste, this is going to be ready in a couple of minutes— will you get the plates out? They're in that cupboard over there. Do you want a fork or chopsticks?'

'A fork, please.' No way was she going to parade her ineptitude with two little sticks in front of him.

'I'll use chopsticks.' She might have known he'd be an expert. 'Just set the table in here, there's no sense in being formal at this time of the night.'

It was a strange meal. There was an ease between them that had never existed before, and yet a tension, too. The meal was simple, yet delicious, the vegetables crisp and gingery and the beef strips amazingly tender in their peanut sauce. When Seven complimented him, Jake told her that he would expect the favour returned and drew her out about some of the weird and wonderful dishes that she remembered some of the circus people preparing on celebration days.

'It would be a great cook-book idea,' she said, 'Cookbooks are among our most often borrowed titles. I used to imagine doing one called "A Circus of Recipes" ...maybe with illustrations of the acts along with the dishes...but I'm not a writer—besides, I never copied any of the recipes down, although I have a very good memory and I can remember watching how my favourites were made.'

'It's a good idea. Worth pursuing. It would make a marvellous soft-cover glossy, if you got the right photographer,' said the shrewd publisher.

Her shyness was instantly triggered. 'Oh, no, I couldn't...it's just something I used to think about, that's all. I wouldn't know how to start...'

He couldn't budge her out of her certainty that such an undertaking would be beyond her acknowledged capabilities. She didn't seem to appreciate that her ability to come up with such an imaginative and innovative concept was half the battle. In the field of non-fiction there were plenty of experts who could help bring her dream to fruition.

Seven was embarrassed by the inadvertent argument she had provoked. She should have realised that an opportunist like Jake looked at everything from the publicity angle. Couldn't he see that going out into the marketplace and selling herself and her idea was out of the question? The mere thought of it froze her to the marrow. Oh, no, she much preferred comfortable anonymity!

The only way she could get the wretchedly stubborn man off his hobby horse was by mentioning that she had spoken to Duncan Hedges that day.

'He called you at the library?' They had loaded the dishes into the dishwasher and moved, with the remainder of the bottle of red wine Jake had opened, back into the lounge. The fire in the grate was burning low and Seven watched Jake poke at it viciously.

'Actually he called in here, about half-past five.'

'What did he want? Scrub that, I know damned well what he wants.' Seven looked at him, puzzled by his vehemence. 'He rang me at the paper this morning.'

'Oh? So you know about the couple from the boarding house being traced to Australia,' murmured Seven. She had been hoping to leave this conversation up to Jake's mother.

'Traced to Sydney airport,' Jake corrected her. 'There's no evidence that that was their final destination.'

'But at least it's a start,' said Seven quietly. Duncan had said his investigation had established that the man and women had been *de facto* partners at the time, not married as they had claimed to the boarding-house owner. He had also discovered that the death of a year-old baby girl belonging to the couple was registered as occurring some months before Rebecca's disappearance. It had been an accidental drowning in a bathtub, and the distraught woman had voluntarily entered a psychiatric institution shortly afterwards. Six months later she was using her dead baby's birth certificate to have an eighteen-month-old daughter added to her passport.

'I suppose Supercop has decided to follow the lead up personally. I understand the weather in Australia is very pleasant this time of year.'

'He couldn't get permission,' Seven said stiffly. 'He said the information has been passed on to Australian police so they can make their own enquiries. He was disappointed because he didn't think they'd assign the case much urgency. I don't know why you're so hostile to Duncan, he's only trying to help.'

'Help himself. He keeps a high profile for a plain clothes detective. He has a reputation among his fellow officers for being too arrogant for his own good, more interested in garnering more glory for himself than building a solid case that'll stand rock-solid in court.'

'How do you know that?'

'I asked around my contacts on the force. He's smooth, Seven, but he's not as reliable as his rank might suggest. Did he by any chance ask you out while he was here?'

'That's none of your business——' Seven began with dignity.

'So he did. I hope you told him where to go. The guy's divorced because he cheated on his wife, although no doubt he told you it was the demands of his job that broke up the marriage...'

Seven blushed. That was exactly what Duncan had told her.

Jake stood before the fire, his hands in his pockets, bristling with contemptuous superiority. 'And you fell for it.'

'I did not!'

'So you're not going out with him,' he confirmed smugly. 'Good girl.'

'I don't need your condescension, thank you,' she told him, half wishing she *had* accepted Duncan's invitation, just to wipe that smug expression off Jake's face. 'I turned him down because he's not my type, that's all. I make my own judgements about people. I'm not a complete innocent, you know.'

'No, I didn't. Aren't you?' he enquired with mock horror. 'Who was he...the man who made you an incomplete innocent?' Her gentle eyes grew even more stormy as he goaded. 'Someone more your type, obviously. What exactly is your type, Seven? How does a man get to qualify?'

'Some never will,' she said meaningfully. 'For a start he would be all the things you're not—gentle, thoughtful, kind, considerate, imaginative, idealistic...'

'All very ethereal, asexual qualities. No man could be all those things all the time and still be a man—just as no woman could and still be a woman. That's only one side of the coin. It's the dark, dominating qualities in us that create the delicious conflict that we call attraction. You see, the softer emotions anyone can pretend to, but the violent, passionate emotions reveal our real, deeper selves. You can mistrust and dislike someone and still find them...' his voice lowered to a rough drawl '... aggravatingly... disturbingly attractive...'

He was almost across the width of the room but Seven felt as if he were only a fluttering heartbeat away. She didn't know whether he was taunting her with his knowledge of her own feelings... or with his, and was afraid that if she tried to make a light, witty reply she would give her uncertainty away. She had no way of knowing that it was written large in her smoke-soft grey eyes and trembling mouth. She looked the essence of innocence at bay, fascinated and yet at the same time fearful of what beckoned.

The exquisite danger of the moment held her spellbound until Jake, not taking his eyes of her, set his half-full glass down on the mantelpiece and took a quietly purposeful step towards her. The single step was enough to break the spell and put her to flight. But on the way to the open door she brushed against the jacket he had earlier tossed on to the back of a chair and knocked it to the floor. His wallet slithered out of the inner pocket and, incurably neat, she automatically bent to pick it and the jacket up, holding them out in front of her like twin shields as she realised her mistake. Jake plucked the jacket away and dropped it carelessly back on to the floor, but his hand wrapped around hers on the slim wallet. She felt the power of him and shivered. Her eyes fell, on to the picture which had become dislodged from its plastic frame and protruded from the cool, snakeskin billfold. A child. Belonging to this man. A child. Love.

The love that father and daughter had shared gripped her, shook her, wouldn't let her go...

'Seven?' He misinterpreted her shaken expression. 'I'm not going to hurt you. I didn't mean what I said the other night...that was the bitterness talking...Seven?' Only when she didn't respond did he realise what held her unwilling attention. She was staring at the half-visible photo of his daughter as if it threatened her in some way. 'It's only Becky—you must have seen her picture before...'

Yes, but not in his presence. The presence of the man who had created a child unknowingly and yet loved her without reservation...nurtured her in his heart and mind for the first short, intense season of her life. A dream and a dread clutched at her.

'I have others, if you'd like to see them. I used to take my own photos when I was in the field so I'm useful with a camera. I have a record of her from the first hour of her life...Becky was such a good subject...'

Seven recoiled, and he held her, addressing gently, alluringly, what he perceived as her vulnerability: 'Come back to the fire and I'll show you. What you said about not having any pictures of your family made me realise how lucky I am. Time will never be able to dim my memory of Becky—whatever happens I still have a very special record of our time together. Wouldn't you like to share that with me...share my sorrow and my need...get to know Becky as I knew her...?'

It was a trap. A sweet but fatal trap. And however much she wanted to feel its blissful bite she knew that for her own sanity's sake she could not let herself share anything with him. Not past, nor present, nor future. He couldn't know what sharing emotions meant for someone like Seven. It meant subjugation, total surrender of herself to her feelings. It meant letting go the fierce self-control that she exercised over her life. It would open the floodgates to an intensity of experience that Jake couldn't even begin to comprehend. Both he and Becky had forced their way too far into her life already...

'No... I won't let you in... either of you,' she murmured distractedly, struggling to reach the safety of the inner core of peace that had always sustained her in times of stress. But Jake sensed her slipping away again and refused to allow her the sanctuary of mental retreat. He dropped the wallet and the gentle attempt at seduction and pulled her hard against him, forcing her to acknowledge the physicality of the moment.

'Deny this, if you can...' he said roughly, and kissed her.

His mouth was like fire, hot and greedy, igniting where it touched and blossoming forth into a blazing conflagration with ravishing speed. Seven's cool resistance was instantly converted into heat, her body melting against his, conforming to his hardness as if he were the mould and she the glowing, molten metal. She was formed and shaped by him, he was the world and everything in it...

His mouth shifted and clung, opening her more completely, his hand cupping her face as a flickering tongue of fire darted inside her, stroking her, consuming and feeding her response until it matched his own. The hand that held hers moved behind her, pinning her wrist to the small of her back, arching her against his aggressive heat. He was hard and full, unashamed of his arousal, moving his hips in slow, thrusting circles that lifted her on to her toes as she tried to ease the ache that the relentless, grinding rhythm created inside her. When he released her captured arm it curled naturally around his clenched shoulders, her fingers spreading out across the tensed muscles, unconsciously kneading his flesh.

He made a dark, harsh sound of satisfaction as he felt the sweet sting of her short, curved nails, and tasted the searing pleasure of her surrender. The hand that cupped her jaw slid to her throat, finding the pounding pulse with a caressing thumb, then moved lower, to shape her breast beneath the unrevealing blouse. A new tension entered her body and he paused in his ruthless exploration of her mouth to whisper soothingly, 'No, don't fight it ... flow with it. Let me show you what you and I were made for...'

His thumb moved again and this time it was her nipple that pulsed against the swirling abrasion, swelling and ripening to a painful tightness within its lace encasement. His mouth dipped and his teeth lightly savaged her tender lower lip with a series of soft bites as he offered the same exquisite caress to her other breast. It was too much... Seven's head tipped back, her eyelids sinking as she moaned a sigh of tormented pleasure, driven to want the dangerous freedom that only minutes ago she had been so afraid of... wanting, *needing* the fulfilment of his bare hands on her naked skin, craving for the first time in her life to be part of someone else.

Her fragile body shook with the violence of her desire.

'Oh, Jake...please...help me...' She meant help her free herself from the constraint of her inexperience, show her how to be wild and wanton and all the things that he wanted her to be, teach her how to be a woman...

But he was only aware that she trembled in his arms, that she felt weak and helpless against his masculine strength. Her eyes when she opened them were dark and bruised with shocked languor, her mouth swollen by his devouring, her hair loosened by his restless fingers into a tangled caramel cloud around her small, flushed and dreamy face.

Suddenly he felt like a brutal seducer. He, who had sought to mercilessly plunder that infuriating innocence, had succeeded all too well. She had stunned him by turning into a slender column of fire in his arms, but now, when the victory was his for the taking, he realised that it would yield only ashes. Whatever Seven's feelings now, she would hate him tomorrow. She was shy, gentle and reserved, and those qualities demanded more than just the swift coupling and quick consummation they were headed for. He wanted her, but not, he realised now, at any cost. It was quite probable, given her natural reticence, that she was still a virgin—in fact he would stake his reputation on it—but it was also obvious that she possessed an intrinsically passionate nature which she refused either to accept or to acknowledge. Her sexuality had ripened with her maturity and yet was still deliciously untried. Up until now her passion had evidently been at the mercy of her prudery, denied any outlet. Jake intended to provide her with one.

The idea of being this woman's first lover, of glutting himself on that first, most sweetest of feminine harvests, was an intoxicatingly heady one. It gratified the primitive male beneath the liberated exterior. It also engendered an erotic desire to protect, to make his desire hers also. Her gentleness deserved a gentle wooing—something that up until this moment he had doubted he was capable of. Now he knew that he was more than capable of it...he would glory in it. She would burn again for him soon, but more fiercely and more enduringly if he took the care to prepare her first. He didn't want her on impulse, he wanted her in the fullness of knowledge. He wanted her as woman to his man, not prey to his hunter; his pride demanded her intellect be involved, as well as her body.

'Jake...' Her brain was beginning to function again and he watched with masochistic satisfaction the confirmation of his wisdom. Fleeting expressions of confusion, desire, horror mingled on her face as she began to realise what had almost happened.

'Well, Seven, do I take it that I might actually qualify after all?' he asked with deliberate mockingness as he opened his hands to let her take flight. 'Or perhaps you're willing to create a special category, just for me...'

She didn't stay to ponder on how suspiciously easy it suddenly was to wrest herself away from the enslavement of passion. She gave him one look of agonised embarrassment and fled.

He didn't follow her physically up the stairs to the sanctuary of the room she shared with her aunt, but his words pursued her like demons.

'You say you want gentle, kind, considerate? Well, mouse, I say you don't really know *what* you want. But whatever it is…I shall see that you have it. I promise…'

CHAPTER SEVEN

SEVEN was in a long corridor, long and bright, so bright it hurt her eyes. There was no colour anywhere. Everything was white. White and cold and silent, and empty. She opened her mouth to cry out but no sound would come. She tried to run but she was rooted to the spot. All she could do was stand and stare along the long, narrowing corridor towards a closed door at the far end. In front of the door was a figure, a smaller version of herself, small and vulnerable, dressed in a billowing white gown. Suddenly the door began to glow an ugly green and she knew... She knew there was something terrible behind that door, something that was going to hurt her, something that she couldn't escape. She couldn't even call out and warn the girl at the door. Terror at her helplessness grew. She could feel the tears pouring down her cheeks and into her mouth, gagging her, suffocating her. She could feel herself shrinking, becoming that girl in front of the tall, terrifying door...

Seven sat up in bed, pressing her shaking hands to her mouth to muffle the strangled sounds in her throat. Her tears were as real as her fears. Her cotton nightdress was drenched with sweat and clung uncomfortably to her trembling body. She took great gulps of air to reassure herself that she was awake...and safe. She slid out of the bed, staggering slightly as her bare feet struck the cold, polished floorboards, reminding her of the barefooted child in the cold corridor. The room was shrouded in darkness, sculpted by even inkier shadows, but the night was kinder than the harsh, frigid lighting of her dream. She could hear her aunt's slow, even breathing punctuating the silence. Quietly, shakily she felt her way to the door and opened it. The upper storey hallway of the house was roofed by steep, sloping windows along the ridgeline and she needed no artificial light to guide her to the luxurious bathroom next door to the old nursery. The moon was a huge, round, pale gold disc suspended in a starry sky above, a friendly, incurious spectator to her uncertain progress.

In the bathroom she couldn't avoid the necessity of turning on the light, and she regarded her image in the mirror wearily as she ran the water to wash her sticky hands and face. Without any make-up she looked like the colourless wraith from her dreams. Her grey eyes were violet with fatigue, the shadows beneath them giving her white face a bruised, wounded quality. Soon not even make-up was going to be able to hide the ravages of her night horrors.

The dreams had started a week ago and had continued to imprint themselves on her subconscious every time she slid into sleep—vivid, frightening and insistent dreams that wouldn't go away.

They had started the night that Jake had taken them to the circus. The disruptive memories that the visit had evoked had triggered the dreams, Seven was sure, but no amount of analysis could bring any meaning to them and that was what frightened her most. It had got to the point where she was almost *afraid* to go to sleep. She read until all hours in bed, the most inoffensive, amicable books that the library stocked, but even they hadn't been sufficiently soothing to quiet her seething subconscious. It just crouched, waiting, biding its time until she was defenceless...

She hadn't wanted to go to the circus, but Charlotte and Aunt Jane had been charmed by Jake's unannounced production of tickets to that evening's performance of a touring American three-ring show. Seven's response had been suspicion, a response that had been justified when Jake had murmured under cover of his mother's almost childlike delight at the novelty, 'What's the matter, Seven? Not *imaginative* enough for you? I thought it rather *thoughtful* and *considerate* of me to take you all out.'

She had blushed, as no doubt he had meant her to, at the reminder of the previous night's indiscretion. He obviously had no intention of letting her draw a discreet veil over what had happened between them.

'But why the circus?' she had asked sullenly.

'Because I thought you'd enjoy it, and the paper was sent extra review tickets...'

'Surely you should give them to an employee with children——' she began rigidly, only to be horrified by her own thoughtlessness as she saw the flickering shock of regret in the navy eyes. 'I... I mean, thank you but I really don't think...I mean I——'

'Calm down, Seven,' he said with a dryness that made her feel even worse. 'It's not a date. You're not going to be alone with me. We'll be well chaperoned...'

'I...it isn't that,' she lied, 'I just don't particularly want to go to the circus——'

Charlotte heard her feeble protest. 'Oh, Seven, you don't meant it? It'll be such fun to see a circus again— I haven't been to one since I was a child. And having an expert like you along to tell us how things are done! Unless...' She faltered. 'Does it hold too many unhappy memories for you, is that why you don't want to come? Of course, we'll understand...' She looked so upset, fumbling for the cigarettes that she seemed to have cut down on lately, in deference to her non-smoking visitors, that Seven didn't have the heart to compound her lies.

'The happy memories far outweigh the bad ones,' she said kindly. 'I just thought that...well, that Jake might prefer to take someone else. I mean, we're not here to...we don't expect to be entertained.'

'Then you expect too little,' he said smoothly, not letting her off the hook. 'Which is almost as bad as expecting too much. Actually I'd prefer to take you on your own, but I knew your over-developed sense of propriety would be offended so I decided to make it a family occasion.'

Aunt Jane's eyes brightened assessingly and Charlotte looked momentarily disconcerted as she stared from her son's bland expression to Seven's flustered guilt. She had never dreamed that he would be so frank about his dishonourable intentions! And the two old women, after they had got over their surprise, were embarrassingly tactful, although Seven had to shake off a stiff interrogation from Aunt Jane later that evening as they got ready to go out.

Seven was stubbornly determined not to enjoy herself at the circus, but her intentions were undermined by the surprising wave of longing that swept over her as they found their places on the ringside benches under the Big Top. The smell of damp ground and sawdust, popcorn and candy-floss, the excited chatter of children mingled with the grouches of some of the adults about the price of everything, the brassy sound of the recorded music that played as the audience filled the seats, the sight of the clowns working the crowd and air of expectation all combined to pull her back into the past. She even felt the same nervous excitement that she used to feel before a performance, a combination of exhilaration and dread.

A big warm hand took possession of her cold one, firm fingers interlacing protectively through hers.

'OK?' It was more than just a simple question, and Seven had to swallow before she could answer without her voice breaking ignominiously.

'Yes, fine.' She didn't try to pull her hand away, partly because she knew Jake had no intention of letting go.

He had held her back to let Aunt Jane and Charlotte move into their seats first, then settled Seven before he sat down himself in the aisle seat. Anyway, his touch was strangely comforting, something to hold on to while her emotions swung back and forth. She glanced gratefully at him and he said quietly, 'If it gets too much for you, let me know. I honestly didn't consider the possibility that it would upset you. This isn't a test, Seven, you don't have to grit your teeth and endure it just because you don't want to spoil anyone else's fun.'

He actually sounded anxious, but by then she had relaxed enough to give him her first completely natural smile, her eyes scrunching into merry crinkles, the way they used to when she was still a carefree child and didn't have to worry about dignity or the lack of it. For a moment Jake had a vision of bright-eyed glee, a little girl to whom merriment was as natural as breathing. He blinked and the vision was gone, and he was looking down at the demure gravity that he was more used to.

'Just looking at that high-wire gives me palpitations,' said Charlotte from beside her, as she stared up in breathless awe at the wire strung between the main supports of the tent. 'Did you ever go up there, Seven, or were you too young...?'

'You're never too young to learn in the circus. Once you've mastered landing in the nets you lose your fear of the height.'

'You actually went on the high wire?' asked Jake, his hand tightening around hers.

'We were a small circus, not like this. Everyone tried a little bit of everything. My mother was a specialist tumbler in a European circus when she met Dad, but when they came back here and started their own show from scratch she learned to do a trapeze act with Boris, who was also our chief clown. She was teaching Morgan and I, too.'

'You must have been a very lively pair,' said Charlotte with a look of loving mockery at her son. 'Unlike *some* children. You know, apart from his flirtation with gymnastics I had to practically *force* Jake out into the world. He was such a quiet boy. I'm sure he only became a journalist, Seven, so that he could thumb his nose at all those years I spent telling him that if he didn't take his nose out of a book life would pass him by. Instead he went right out and made reading and writing his profession!'

Jake as a bookish youth? Seven looked at him in amazement. He met her look with a sardonic smile of understanding.

'Did you think I was the ultimate swaggering, macho adolescent?' he jibed softly, and laughed when she blushed at having her glib assumptions neatly exposed. 'I'm afraid I was the romantic, languishing intellectual type... quite the *idealist* until life taught me otherwise. But I'm sure, given sufficient incentive, I could dredge up the remnants of that pallid affectation....' His dark eyes taunted her with the shared secret of what that incentive might be.

Further conversation was thwarted by the dimming of the lights, and Seven settled back to enjoy the show. As she had expected, it was extremely slick and professional, with lots of American razzmatazz. It was a long time, too long, since she had allowed herself the pleasure of going to the circus, and she found her perspective altered. She no longer viewed it with the detached appreciation of an 'insider'. Tonight she was gripped by the glamour and the thrills, all the things that she had kidded herself she was too cynical and mature to be conned by. Tonight she didn't see the sweat and tears that went on behind the scenes, tonight she laughed, and gasped, and clapped with everyone else, letting her disbelief gracefully go for the duration. Tonight she was happy.

At the first break Charlotte insisted on going out to try her hand at one of the fairground attractions that cluttered the small entrance-tent, and Aunt Jane, with a meaningful look at Seven, went with her.

Ignoring the look, Seven tried to rise, but Jake's shifting legs stopped her.

'Don't go. Why spoil their evening?'

'You know what they think?'

'I know that your aunt sees the glister of gold in her crystal ball. She thinks that you might soften me up with your winsome smiles...'

'It's your fault,' she told him flatly. 'You're the one who hinted——'

'Am I complaining?' he asked her. 'I don't see why I should hide the fact that I find you attractive, as if it's something to be ashamed of.'

'You mean you're not ashamed to be seen with the niece of a crazy old woman?' she asked tartly.

'I'm not ashamed to be seen with *you*,' he said gently. 'You're looking very beautiful this evening...'

'There's no need to go overboard,' she said, jerking her eyes away, not wanting to see the mockery in his. His hand under her chin tipped her head back.

'I mean it. That blue dress reflects in your eyes—makes them look like lavender-grey morning skies, all soft and billowy with promise. And although you were silly to pull your hair back like that, I like the way the light gilds it with warmth, so that it's like a twist of flowing caramel.' His words were soft, and liquid with warmth, a seduction in themselves. 'And I like the purity of line in your face, the starched contours covered by that lovely clear skin. And most of all I like to see you laugh. Gravity suits you, but so does laughter. When you laugh it melts away all those incipient worry lines that you're in danger of developing here...' His fingertip traced the translucent silkiness between her brows. 'And here...' The warm, tingling touch brushed down from her nose to her mouth. Now he *was* teasing, but it was a very seductive form of teasing that invited her disbelief. In the back of those navy eyes was a small, intense glow that flattered her far more than his wickedly beautiful words. *Now* she could believe him as the studious intellectual, the dreamer, the romantic gleaner of words. And yet, he was the tough, cynical journalist, too, the exposer and derider of dreams... The combination was dangerous... exciting... Seven's eyes almost swallowed her face as she followed her thoughts to their natural conclusion. She felt as if she had stepped on to the high wire for the first time, and suddenly noticed that someone had taken the safety net away. Such would be the risk of loving Jake Jackson!

Even more disturbing was his next comment. 'I know you think you're happy in your little library, keeping the big bad world at bay, but I don't think you are, not really. You're content, which is a different thing altogether. Contentment can be stultifying. Happiness demands progress, change, to be complete, to grow... It requires you to reach out and take it. Your aunt, for instance, is happy; she throws herself completely into everything she does, good and bad. You, on the other hand, are always holding something back, something in reserve. I think it's that part of you that's here. The child part, the circus part, the fun part...'

'That's ridiculous,' she said dismissively. 'I enjoy watching the show but that doesn't mean I want to be part of it——'

'That's not what I meant. It must have been difficult for you, trying to fit in with your aunt after having all this as a playground...' He indicated the rings with a sweeping hand. 'I think you succeeded by ruthlessly shutting the door on your old life and making a completely fresh start. That's why you're so averse to change now, why you like everything so neat and tidy and in its place, because it reassures you that *you* have a place.

You're so wary, so careful not to appear frivolous, as if you're afraid the world will fall to pieces if you act spontaneously. It won't. In fact you might find it a sweeter place to be, and far less complicated and hostile than you might imagine...'

'You're just inventing a story around a few flimsy facts,' she said shakily. 'Making something interesting out of nothing. But then, I suppose that's called journalistic licence.' Deliberately goading him, she added, 'If you're looking for a sensational story you should be talking to Aunt Jane, not me.'

'Should I?' he murmured, with frightening mildness, his eyes narrowing thoughtfully as they searched out and settled on the sharp-faced old lady with her ridiculously black hair and vividly clashing clothes as she made her way back along the rows, his mother following, her face animated with a serene amusement. 'Madame Zoe is all flash and dash, and I admit I haven't figured out how she manages to sometimes be uncannily accurate with her predictions and at others so laughably wrong... I can't help but feel that all that slightly crazy superficiality hides nothing more than...a slightly crazy superficiality. I find it hard to stay angry with her for her ridiculous posturing, particularly since her peculiar brand of amusement seems to have lifted Mother out of the doldrums. Or perhaps it's because she's your aunt that I can forgive her...'

Thank goodness the clowns came tumbling back at that point, but Seven was aware that her laughter was pitched a little high at their antics, and that Jake watched her as often as he did the rest of the performance...

The circus had only been the beginning. The next evening Jake had arrived home with Press passes for the theatre, and the evening after that it had been tickets for a concert. With his mother and her aunt in tow Seven could enjoy Jake's company without feeling guilty. After all,

they weren't actually *dating*...although somehow
Charlotte and Jane always seemed to find the occasion
to wander off and leave the younger generation to their
own devices. To Seven's slight bewilderment, and secret
chagrin, Jake behaved like the perfect gentleman she
knew he wasn't—he flirted but he never touched, he was
wickedly provocative but he never carried through, he
prowled like a tom-cat around her with his questions but
never settled on one subject long enough for her to
become uncomfortable. His curiosity was as wide-
ranging as it was insatiable, and she began to understand why he was such a good journalist.

By the time Jake whisked her off on her own, for a
rare books exhibition at the Auckland Museum, Seven
was imbued with the comfortable illusion that she was
handling the demon publisher without too much effort.
Fortunately she didn't realise that her illusion was sustained only by a massive effort on *his* part.

Exploring the wondrous library of beautiful old books
amassed by a Wellington collector Seven was in her
element and, for the first time, was totally relaxed in
Jake's company. This was one subject in which she could
be certain she was more knowledgeable than he, and she
subtly made it known as she led him around the glass
cases. Jake found her gentle arrogance enchantingly
amusing, but he put on an obligingly humble face as he
listened to her enthusiasm carry her away. Later they
walked through the hilly park surrounding the museum,
holding hands because, as Jake pointed out, the blustery
wind on the exposed hillside was strong enough to blow
her away. They bought hot chips at the kiosk by the
duckpond to warm their insides and fed the remains to
the eager ducks when it began to rain. They rushed back
to the car and tumbled, wet and laughing, inside.

'Winter and you suit each other,' Jake said suddenly
and, still laughing, Seven replied flippantly,

'Because we're both cold and wet?'

'No, because you complement each other,' he said quietly, and brushed a raindrop from her cheek with a gesture that obliterated all the meaningless touches that had come before it. 'In the midst of all this grey and stormy turbulence you shine with a warm, quiet lustre that many more striking women would envy. You're like a fragile shaft of sunlight, a small piece of calm at the eye of a storm...'

'How boring.' Seven faltered, trembling at his sudden seriousness, thinking of all the 'more striking,' and exciting women he must know.

'Oh, no. Not boring...' He sipped the raindrop from his finger, tasting it with a deliberation that made her blush. 'Welcoming...'

He didn't say any more, but it was enough. He wanted her to welcome him. The next move must be hers.

Unfortunately Jake's company had had another, even more compelling effect on her. Her increased sensitivity to his thoughts and feelings had resolved the vague, meaningless moments of fleeting premonition into sharp focus, forcing her to give them credence. She had been speaking the truth when she had told her aunt that she couldn't force precognition, but she could, and had been, unconsciously repressing it, trying to hold herself aloof. Now she had to face her fears.

She dried her face on the thick, fluffy white guest towel and turned away. Clicking off the bathroom light, she made her way back down the hall, but walked past her own room without hesitating. The night was crisp with winter chill but Seven didn't feel it, as she opened the door to Rebecca's room, her concentration already turning inwards. Her long, white nightdress with its embroidered sweetheart neckline gleamed palely in the dimness, the parts of it that were still damp clinging to her legs as she walked.

She turned on the night-light which was plugged into the wall beside the bookcase. Its glow was faint, subdued, like her senses as she moved around the room in a dreamy trance, touching objects, setting a little ballerina music-box in motion, brushing a fingertip against a nursery-rhyme mobile that hung above the empty cot.

She began to hum a nameless tune and her feet began to dance, a slow, uncertain, whirling dance of doubtful grace. Her hands and feet tingled, her mind was filled with lightness, and for a moment she floated on the brink of joy. But then the tendrils of fear began to creep. It seemed they grew from the bare boards upwards, twining around her legs so that she began to stumble, wrapping tighter, reaching up towards her throat to choke her. Her head, which had been dizzily light, was suddenly too heavy, pushing down on her fragile body. She swayed, turning around and around, trying to unwind the horrible, cold snaking coils that tightened around her. She whirled faster and faster, crying out in her fear, a raw contrast to the sweet tinkle of the music box. The harsh light that had so frightened her in her dream blinded her again, but this time there was a shadow in the middle of the brightness, a dark outline that made her sob with relief.

'Daddy!' She held out her hands in terror that he would vanish and leave her alone again in the bright emptiness.

The outline moved and suddenly it was solid, and real, and all around her, enveloping her with warmth and the familiar loving male scent.

'Daddy!' she sobbed, clutching at him frantically.

'It's all right, sweetheart, you're having a nightmare, that's all... Come back to bed...' The rumbling reassurance only terrified her more. He didn't understand. He was going to put her in that bed and go away again. But it wasn't a nightmare, it was *real*!

'No, it hurts, Daddy, it *hurts*!' Her little hands kneaded him painfully. 'Make it stop, Dada-Jay. Star-kisses for Becksa!'

Jake stiffened. He arched violently away from the trembling woman in his arms but Seven wouldn't let him go, her face still buried in his chest. Jake swore and wound a savage hand into the damp curls that sprayed across the front of his black robe. He pulled her head back viciously, his eyes raking her tear-stained face. Her eyes were tight shut against the overhead light which he had flicked on when he had entered the room.

'Seven, wake up!'

She frowned and whimpered and he shook her head with his painful grip.

'Don't, Daddy, my head hurts.'

'Seven, wake up.' This time he accompanied his harsh command with a stinging slap on her cheek. He didn't give a damn about the warnings about waking a sleep-walker gently. If this was a sick game he had no intention of playing.

Tears welled from under her sealed lids above the reddened mark on the baby-smooth cheek. 'Daddy!' The gasp wrenched the guts out of him. He gritted his teeth as her eyes trembled, lifted, to reveal a wealth of pain and sorrow and reproach.

He was insane.

He was in a nightmare of his own.

Her eyes were wide and childlike.

'You hit me!' She pouted, that strange woman-child whose face was suddenly formless around those devastating eyes.

Jake felt the horror lock every bone and sinew. Every cell in his body recoiled from the thing in his arms and yet he couldn't let her go.

'I'm sick!' she said, in a little plaintive whine. 'My head hurts, and my neck…and I'm hot…I'm burning.' She pushed her face at him, nuzzling aside his robe and sighing as she found his cool, bare chest. The heat she was generating was phenomenal.

'Seven——' His voice was thick and strange to his ears.

'Not seven,' she giggled sadly. 'I'm eight. I just had my birthday, remember...why did you only give me two candles, Dada-Jay? I'm a big girl now.' Her voice crept lower with every word until he hardly heard. 'He hurt me.'

'Who hurt you?' Jake gagged on the question that ripped out of his throat.

'He did.'

'Who? Who hurt you, Becky?' He cupped her small chin and turned up her drooping head.

'He did. He said it would make me feel better but it didn't. Why didn't you come, Dada-Jay? I missed you. Where did you go?'

'Where did *you* go, Becky?'

'Big...' she said sleepily in a high, childish voice.

'Big what?' He resisted the urge to shout, to shake her. 'Where are you, Becky? Tell Dada-Jay... Are you in a house? Here, look——' He lifted one of her hands and spread it out with his and kissed each of the cold, white fingertips. 'Star-kisses for Becksa. Everything'll be all right now, sweetheart, just tell me where you are...'

She smiled sleepily, blinking, tears gone, but Jake saw that the childishness was gone too, as if it had only been a trick of the light...

She mumbled something that meant nothing. 'Tired. Sleep now...s'awright now...'

'No, you can't sleep! Don't go to sleep.' He did shake her then, but it was too late. Her head lolled like a rag doll's on her stiffly angled neck. 'Oh, God, Becky...' He buried his face in her ragged curls, letting his own tears be absorbed by the caramel silk. When she began to struggle, it wasn't the feeble resistance of a tired child, it was the the panicky strength of a woman.

'Don't, Jake, what do you think you're doing——?' Seven's exclamation was cut off when she saw his face, the man's tears. 'Jake? What's wrong? What's happened? Is it your mother——?'

'Don't you know?'

'Know?' She suddenly became aware of their surroundings. Hazy memory stirred. Oh, dear God, what had she done?

'It's you, isn't it? Not your aunt. No wonder the pieces refused to fall into place. It's *you*!' Shock turned to uncertainty, which was even more unbearable than the certainty of loss. Ruthlessly Jake dredged for the protection of rage. 'The whole thing has been a grotesque lie. And the hellish irony of it is that I knew it! The mistake I made right back at the beginning—it wasn't really a mistake after all!'

'Jake——'

Her soft plea triggered an explosion. He shook her violently, his voice stripped raw with hatred and despair. 'Why the charade, Seven? Why? Do you like to draw the thing out to make it worth more? To make me more *grateful*? God, I can't believe it . . . all this time, I was watching your aunt, and you were the one. Is that the reason for all the lies . . . so you can snoop around and get the information you need while Madame Zoe provides the distraction?'

'No—Jake——' His hands tightened around her slender upper arms, but the pain was nothing to that in her heart.

'I suppose you wormed Becky's baby-name for me out of Mother, and that little titbit about star kisses on her fingers. It's all a game to you, isn't it, you callous little bitch? And you'll use anything and anyone without compunction.' He gave a savage laugh. 'And to think I flattered myself I understood you, I felt sorry for you— the shy Miss Mouse who needed to be treated softly, gently. How many have you suckered with *that* lie? God, you even have a cop in the palm of your sweetly grasping hand . . . no wonder you didn't buckle under my threats. You're completely amoral, aren't you? In fact I wouldn't be surprised to find out that your senile old aunt is just a pawn in your game, a convenient front to hide behind, someone to take the flak for you, someone to take the blame. Well, this time you've over-reached yourself. I may have been a sucker but I'm not an enduring one. I realise that this timely little performance of yours was supposed to be the clincher——'

'I—it wasn't a performance, Jake. I...I didn't know you were there——' she choked, battered by his outpouring of contempt.

'No? You expect me to believe that? From you, the consummate liar? How far were you prepared to go, Seven, to get *me* on your side? Would you have gone to bed with me? That's where we were heading, weren't we? An intense little affair to cement loyalties... Damn you, Seven, you treacherous bitch. You really came close. I actually *believed* in you!'

It was, she realised later, a cry of disillusioned self-contempt. The great investigative journalist, the hardened cynic who was invulnerable against the wiles of the world, had been duped as easily as a child. He had been suspicious and wary, and yet still he had succumbed to the illusion of...of what? Of innocence in a befouled world? Was that how he had seen her? As a symbol of what he had lost? Certainly it had not been an illusion of love, not for him. In all his fine, writer's words he had never come close to mentioning love. No, if the truth be known he was using her quite as callously as he thought she had been using him, for the excitement of—what was it?—an intense little affair? He had thought that she was shy and innocent and yet he had tried to seduce her!

But it didn't work, she discovered, shivering in her own bed several hours later. She couldn't find any strength in anger because she knew how he had felt. She had experienced his bitterness as if it was her own...as perhaps it was. She had seen the shock of utter betrayal in his eyes before it had been superseded by restorative rage. Beneath that rich vein of emotionalism Jake was a deeply committed man. He was committed to facts, to logic. However he manipulated them for the sake of sensation, at rock-bottom he was a journalist from the old school—a mystery was just a story waiting to be written, waiting for someone to dig up the facts that would explain it all, answer all the questions. Only Seven was a mystery that no questions could unravel because no one, not even she, had the answers. Her very existence defied the sacred 'facts', and that was something that Jake would never, never accept.

Seven was always alone, but now, tonight, she felt more isolated than ever. She had gone back to her room, ripped off her nightgown and pulled on some clothes, stuffing the rest of her things into her suitcase.

Aunt Jane, jolted from her conscienceless sleep, had reacted in typical fashion by refusing to believe that they had to leave, especially in the middle of the night.

'Don't be ridiculous, Seven. I'm not getting out of a warm bed to run off like a thief in the night! It's freezing out there. I might catch a chill and you know how colds always run to my chest. If he was angry I'm sure that in the morning he'll be over it. Besides, maybe it's a good thing that he knows the truth.'

It would have been useless arguing with the stubborn old woman, so Seven hadn't tried. She had rushed out to her car and driven recklessly home. At the time she hadn't cared about anything but getting away. Now, sleepless and cold with despair in the empty old house, she had time to worry. Surely Jake wouldn't hurt Aunt Jane—not if he thought that she was just Seven's dupe? Or was he so full of black rage that he would lash out at whoever was nearest? And what about Charlotte, who at the circus seemed to have acquired a new enthusiasm for life, had talked about the past with fond reminiscence rather than anguish...? Seven's tears came slow and hard, but this time there was no warm, comforting body to rock her. And there wouldn't be, ever. She was what she was, and if the man she loved couldn't accept that how could she hope to inflict it on anyone else?

It was nearly dawn before her eyelids began to droop over her hot, aching eyes, only to spring open again at the thunderous banging. She hadn't bothered to turn on the oil heater when she had flung into the house and now she regretted it. The air on her face was like a cold mask. A mist thickened the dawn, and when she sat up to look out of her window she could see an icy crust glistening on the small back lawn. She huddled in bed, hoping that the banging would soon stop, but without much real faith. She knew very well who it was. Only Jake Jackson would have no compunction about waking the whole neighbourhood to get his way. The more public her humiliation, the better, as far as he was concerned! At last, when the banging transferred to her back door, accompanied by shouting, she got up, her hands shaking as she pulled on her thick red robe. It was very old, a line around the hem showing where it had been let down as she grew. She had had this gown with her on the night of the fire and over the years had handled it with the greatest care, glad that it was made of a thick, pure wool that resisted wear. It was her security blanket, her legacy, her comfort, and she hugged it around her now as she padded through the kitchen to the back door, which was vibrating with the pounding it was receiving.

'Seven? Is that you?' Jake's voice demanded as she turned on the light and fumbled with the security lock. 'Open this damned door. Now! Or I'll kick it in!'

CHAPTER EIGHT

JAKE didn't give Seven time to open the door. As soon as he heard the latch click he thrust at the barrier with an angry hand, slamming the door open and storming inside, just the way that he had on that first, memorable occasion. He certainly looked every bit as menacing, if not more so, in a bulky woollen sweater that increased the width of his powerful shoulders, and a pair of dark trousers that were pulled tight across his strong thighs and lean hips. His dark hair was a mess and the unshaven jaw jutted threateningly. He looked like hell, come to call.

Seven, clutching her robe, took a step back, trembling. 'What do you want?' Unfortunately her demand came out as an uncertain quaver. She tried again. 'How dare you come around here and wake me up and harass me?'

'You were asleep?' He sounded incredulous and she glared at him.

'Of course I was,' she lied furiously. 'But you were making enough racket to wake the dead. You're lucky someone didn't call the police—you're lucky *I* didn't call the police, but then a heartless criminal like me wouldn't want to attract the attention of the law, would I?'

She expected him to lash out equally furiously in reply. Instead the midnight eyes flickered, fell, roamed her red-clad figure and finally closed. He tipped his head back and took a deep breath, his chest rising steeply under the cream wool. When his eyes found hers again she was shaken by the tenderness that had enveloped the burning anger.

'Becky had a warm sleep robe just like that,' he said huskily, his mouth twisting as he added, 'Except hers had feet in it.'

Seven's bare toes curled against the bare vinyl. She had packed in such a hurry she had forgotten to retrieve the slippers from under her bed. 'I'm not your daughter,' she said harshly, rejecting the olive-branch.

'But you were. Back there in her room for a few moments, you *were* Becky.'

'No,' Seven whispered, taking another step back. He had come because of his daughter. It was Becky he wanted, not Seven.

He followed. 'Yes. I was there. I saw...I heard.'

'But you didn't believe——'

'I don't know what I believe any more,' he said softly, holding her eyes with his as he edged closer. 'But I know what you believe. And I know that I hurt you...'

'No.' It was important that she denied it. That he didn't realise how much he could hurt her.

'Yes. I meant to. It's what I've wanted all along. To hurt you. To deny what you mean to me...'

Her eyes opened hugely. 'I...I'm a way to find your daughter.'

He shook his head, and took another step closer to her mesmerised figure. 'You're a way to find me, the man I could be...the man I was when I had somebody of my own to love...'

'No——' Tears blinded her. She knew what it was that she wanted him to mean. She wanted it so badly that her mind had convinced her it was true.

'Yes.' He caught the defensive hand she pushed out and raised it to his lips, kissing the curled fingertips. 'I used to do this for Becky when she was a baby, when she had hurt herself. I called them star-kisses because her fists were like little stars. It used to make her laugh, even through her tears. And Dada-Jay was her special name for me. I used to take her to work with me some-

times, and she heard people calling me J.J. Jay was her
first word, even before the Dada part. I haven't let myself
think about those things for a very long time. That's
why I reacted so badly back there—you suddenly made
Becky real for me again, I couldn't cope. Hit and run,
I've got good at that. It's how I run my paper, how I
run my life. All because I'm afraid, afraid of loving,
afraid of losing. I live in a world of emotional throw-
aways. It's tough, at my age, to face the notion that my
entire premise for life might be wrong...'

'You shouldn't do that——' Seven choked, staring
helplessly at his mouth as he took her other lifeless hand
and lifted it to the hard curve of his lips. Each fingertip
he kissed, and then sucked gently, in a way that she was
sure he had never soothed his daughter. It was
so...erotic. Her toes curled even more tightly.

'I must. Forgive me?'

'I——' She had prepared herself for battle and he had
slid under the barricades with pathetic ease, 'I...you
can't just barge in here and...and...'

'Beg your forgiveness? I don't expect you to make it
easy for me, little mouse. You have every right to rub
my nose in it. You were only trying to help me, and I
drove you out into the snow with my wild, selfish
accusations——'

'D...don't be ridiculous, it isn't snowing, it's only a
frost...' she stammered, bewildered by his humbleness,
wondering if it was some kind of trap. 'Are you wired
or something?'

His eyebrows rose. 'I never take drugs.'

'I meant have you got a tape running or something?
Maybe you've got a brace of photographers lurking out
there waiting to pounce in when you've manoeuvred me
into a sufficiently compromising position——'

His eyes sparked with brief humour. 'I only wish I
could.' He sobered when he saw how close she was to
believing her own desperate defence. 'Seven, I'm alone

and unarmed. I'm not even carrying a pencil. I drove around for hours after our... *my* fight, thinking, trying to pluck up the courage to go home and make my peace with you. Only to find, when I got back, that you'd gone. Your aunt said——'

'You spoke to Aunt Jane?' Seven tried to free her hands to hide her burning cheeks, but Jake was relentless.

'I think it would better fit the facts to say that she spoke to me,' he said wryly. 'She was very put out that I accused her of using you——'

'You accused *her* of using *me*?' Seven lit up angrily at the memory. 'You've certainly changed your tune—— '

'I told you, I had hours to think... You're such a private person, you try so hard to be small and unnoticed, tolerant of everyone but yourself... So restrained and yet so emotional, sensitive to the slightest nuance of feeling. How terrible that must be, to be so open...'

His fingers were threading caressingly in and out of hers, holding her still for the devastating gift of his understanding.

'You think it's a trick——'

'I know that my mother didn't tell you about the star-kisses, or about Becky calling herself Becksa. Oh, yes, I spoke to her, too—or rather she joined in Jane's tirade against me. She wasn't altogether surprised that *you* were the source of the information rather than your aunt. It seems I'm the only one who was so wilfully blind.' His grip tightened momentarily. 'I suppose even that faithless Romeo is in on the secret——'

'If you mean Duncan, no he isn't,' Seven roused herself to protest.

'Oh? Not such a good cop after all,' Jake smirked.

'*Jake*——'

He lifted their clasped hands to her lips. 'No, let me finish. I've never believed in the possession of paranormal powers, but I have no option but to accept that you have some mental link with my daughter, and that it is agonisingly real to you. If I accept that reality then I must also face the wider contradiction. I'm a realist, but so are you, mouse, even if you don't recognise it. Because of that I think that you have as much difficulty as I in believing in your "magical" power to connect your mind with that of a total stranger. And that powerful resistance within you is what compels *my* belief. If you embraced it with the enthusiasm that Madame Zoe does I would be far more suspicious. But how can I suspect someone so loath to take advantage of such a stupendous gift? Because that's what it is, Seven. A gift, not a curse... that's how you see it sometimes, isn't it? As an invasion of yourself, your private self. I couldn't bear it, but you can, and do... Ah, mouse, you can't share the gift but you can share the pressures that it burdens you with. All you have to do is let go...'

She looked at him in horror. With one hand he offered her the exquisite balm of his understanding and with the other he snatched it away. How could he say such an appalling thing? Ask her to place herself in his hands, hands that had wanted to tear her apart only a few hours... lifetimes... ago? If he asked that of her he couldn't really believe in her 'gift', but he was prepared to suspend disbelief just to get what he wanted: information about his daughter. And then, when he had what he wanted, he would bring the full weight of that rational mind to bear in order to push her away.

'Go away. I don't want you here,' she said in a voice as cold as the frost outside, her eyes lifeless grey stones in her stricken face.

He looked at her and smiled. The curve of his mouth was hard and purposeful. 'You don't want me as much as I don't want you,' he told her with the ironic softness of utter certainty, pulling her slowly into his body. 'You don't want me so much you tremble every time I come within speaking distance.' Seven strained backwards but his strength swallowed hers with stunning ease. She was gathered in his hands, held, taunted with the obviousness of what she so strenuously denied. Her generous breasts flattened against the rough wool of his sweater, her waist was encircled by an inexorable arm and drawn to the tautness of his belly, her hips imprinted by his muscled thighs. Everything about him was tense, hard, leashed with a tightly coiled expectancy.

'Jake, I can't——'

'You can,' came his murmur in the graceful curve of her throat as she leaned back to fight her rearguard action. 'You can and you will...you know you will, that's why you're so frightened. You know the battle's lost even before it's begun...' The last was whispered against her lips. 'Give it up, darling, before you hurt yourself...'

Seven couldn't think. The small, biting kisses he was pressing against her mouth absorbed all of her attention. Every automatic function of her body suddenly went haywire; even breathing required a conscious act of will. Each time his mouth moved she forgot something new, and it never seemed to stop moving. The known universe was suddenly no larger than a man.

His hands, which had been cool, were like hot brands as they bound her to him, massaging the layers of her clothing against her sensitive skin, making her burn where they touched. His mouth, warm and moist and dizzyingly clever, devoured the rags of her resistance, the rocking undulation of the masculine hardness against her slender body rousing a sweet turmoil within. She arched, no longer in protest, but in pleasure, welcoming his intricate, erotic exploration. The slow-burning fuse of her emotions suddenly erupted in a shower of sparks. Seven, who had barely skimmed the surface of her sexuality during her wary forays into romance, was plunged to the wild, tumultuous depths, and shot to the heavens within the space of a heartbeat.

To Jake the experience was heady beyond belief. His penchant for strong, assertive woman had given him plenty of experience with women who liked to seize the initiative in lovemaking but he had never felt as ravished as he did now, by a tiny, trembling thing whom he could break with one hand tied behind his back. She was still tiny, she still trembled, but nevertheless she dominated him with pure sensual delight. He adjusted her against him and groaned at the soft insinuation of her curves, splaying his legs so that he could move her sensuously between them to assuage the savage ache in his loins, and regretting it when he almost exploded with premature pleasure.

'Dear God, mouse...' he gritted through clenched teeth, inhaling the fragrant warmth of her arousal as he buried his face in her throat. 'Slow down or I'll take you now, before you're ready...'

Not *ready*? Seven struggled in blind astonishment, her hip grazing his hardness in a way that made him groan afresh. Somehow her robe had become untied and the neatly buttoned bodice of her modest gown pulled down to expose the upper curves of her breasts. Surely he wasn't going to stop *now* out of some sort of misguided sense of chivalry?

'No, I don't mean that...' He laughed rawly as he lifted his head and caught sight of her flushed dismay. He ran a possessive hand down the length of her spine, and over her buttocks, tucking them impossibly closer to the source of his agony. 'I meant here, on the floor. And I don't want to do that. I'd be afraid of crushing your bones.' He shuddered unwillingly. 'I'm half afraid of it anyway. You feel so delicate...so small...too small to accommodate me. Sex with me might shatter you to pieces...'

His lip-service to caution was revealed as just that when Seven managed to whisper in a dream of delight, 'Oh, yes...Jake...shatter me...'

He surged against her, jolted by the kick her words delivered to his ego and his libido. 'You've never done this before, have you, mouse? Given yourself to a man?'

She stiffened. 'Does it matter?'

'Only in that I think your first time should be in the proper place...in a bed...with a man who cares enough to make it beautiful for you...' he murmured, kissing away her fear with greedy enjoyment that told her that he had no intention of denying either of them. 'Show me where you sleep, Seven... Take me to your bed...'

The invitation was sinfully exciting, but not easy to fulfil. He wouldn't let her go; each swaying step required a kiss, a touch, a sweet caress, a murmur of pleasured encouragement. By the time they reached her bedroom neither of them could have gone another step. Jake kissed her once more, slowly, thoroughly, and then let her go so that he could strip off his sweater. She laid her hands against his bared chest, feeling the thunderous leap of his heart, and his eyes gleamed in the soft yellow light from the bedside lamp.

'See what you do to me?' he growled with an indrawn breath that moved his chest caressingly against her flattened hands. 'Now, let me see what I do to you...' And he tugged away her nightgown, sliding it down her shoulders, drawing her arms with it until it was caught by the flowering of her hips, her hands trapped in the folds. The look in his eyes as he studied her bare breasts for the first time made her blush madly and he smiled, watching her shiver as he cupped her silken ripeness.

'I see I excite you,' he said huskily, his hands contracting so that the stinging points of her nipples dragged against his palms. 'So sweet...so sensitive. I wondered whether your acute mental sensitivity was matched by a physical one. Shall we find out...?' He bent his head, lifting his cupped hands, and Seven was shocked with the wonder of watching him taste her. His tongue stroked over her creamy flesh, making it glisten with pleasure, and when at last the hot lash flicked over her swollen nipple she cried out. But that pleasure was nothing to the hot gush of satisfaction she felt when he drew the dewy peak into his mouth and began to softly suckle. A red mist exploded behind her eyes and her legs gave way, her body sagged and she gave a soft moan of frustration as the involuntary action momentarily denied her the exquisite torture of that moist, rhythmic tugging. But it was only momentarily, for Jake followed her down on to the bed and continued to worship the taut peaks until Seven finally managed to free her hands, tearing the nightgown in the process, and plunge a weak hand into the thick dark hair that hid his intent face from her. She wrenched his head up and for a moment they stared at each other, breathless. To her astonishment a dark flush spread across Jake's face.

'I'm sorry,' he said shakily, his hand moving from the lushness of her breast to remove her entangled hand from his hair and draw it against his chest which, under the thick frost of hair, was slick with sweat. 'Was I hurting you?'

She shook her head wordlessly, her hair flowing against the chaste whiteness of her pillow, unable to suck in enough oxygen to answer him.

'You *are* sensitive...' he murmured with greedy satisfaction, his eyes on the quivering promise of her lower lip. 'Exquisitely so... I'll be more gentle, I promise...'

She shook her head again and his lids narrowed. 'Too much...' she gasped. 'It's too...like, like...falling...I felt...I felt...'

His slitted eyes were as black as sin as he guided her faltering courage back on to its predetermined path. 'What you're supposed to feel. I was falling too, mouse, only faster... When it gets too much you don't pull back...you *jump*!' With a soft, tearing sound he dragged the nightgown from her hips and put his hands around her slender waist, his thumbs stroking down across her tender belly, feeling the deep muscles there quiver and contract. He rolled briefly on to his back to strip his belt from its tabs and remove the rest of his clothes with a breathtakingly erotic economy of movement, and then he was over her again, kissing her, urging her against his hair-roughened chest and thighs, inviting her to re-discover the mindless sensual paradise she had hesitated to enter, rewarding each tiny step forward with im-measurable delight. It wasn't long before the heated rhythm had re-established itself and she was demanding more from him than his promise permitted him to give. He held back as long as was humanly possible, his body straining savagely against its self-imposed bonds, but he wasn't proof against the blatant seduction of her in-nocence, against the shocked expression of wide-eyed wonder and gasps of bliss that greeted each bold new venture. And the moment his hardness slipped between her satiny thighs, teasing at the soft, feathery cradle that rocked the heart of her, was his last moment of even near-coherent thought. No longer gentle teacher and ardent pupil, no longer strong leading weak, masculine invading feminine, they merged as equals, not falling but rising, ever faster, higher, harder, until the primitive power that propelled them exploded in a final, violent burst of glory.

Afterwards he lay on her heavily, not moving, cover-ing her, his head turned away.

'Jake?' She was afraid of what his concealed face hid. Disappointment? Regret?

He was silent, his slick, hot body lax on top of her. She felt her heart shiver. He had said he cared, not that he loved, but she had thought it would be enough...a beginning. 'Jake?'

He turned his head, slowly, sliding sideways to lie beside her on the narrow bed. 'Seven...' He touched her bruised mouth with a gentle finger, his eyes dark with compassion and...

Shame! He was *ashamed*! Seven recoiled, knocking his hand away, suddenly excruciatingly aware of her nudity—and his... They had fallen on to the top of the bedspread, so there was no concealing sheet to tug around her. She looked around frantically, but there was only her shredded nightdress lying accusingly on the floor.

'Seven, no——' He flung his arm across her waist as she tried to scoot off the bed. 'Don't run away. For goodness' sake, Seven, you can't judge sex by your first time, give it a chance... There won't be any pain next time, it will be better, I promise...'

He was babbling. Jake, the seasoned wordsmith. Seven stopped trying to escape the iron clamp around her narrow waist. She stared at him over her shoulder, and for the second time in an hour she saw him flush. Her eyes widened. Jake was embarrassed! He was pleading for a second chance to please her! He had so completely lost control, he really didn't *know*... She should put him out of his misery now.

Keeping her body still half turned from his, she said slowly, 'Th...there wasn't any pain this time.'

He looked disconcerted. 'Then why...?' His flush suddenly became a pallor. 'Is it just me? You didn't like what I did?' He shifted uneasily, his fingers digging unconsciously into the bony curve of her hip. Seven couldn't help noticing that even in the confused aftermath of their lovemaking he was still semi-aroused...either that or he was simply very well endowed. She suspected, remembering the feel of him inside her, that it was both! She blushed bright red at her thoughts and he, mistaking it for awkwardness at the intimacy of their conversation, continued quickly, 'I rushed...I thought you were with me all the way...I forgot that it was all new to you.' Another appalling idea struck him. 'I know you're a modest little thing, maybe I shouldn't have done some of the things I did your first time. For God's sake, Seven, say something—tell me I didn't turn you off!'

His anxiety was so ludicrous that Seven couldn't help it, she giggled. He snatched his arm away as if she had stung him and sat up, magnificent in his naked affront. 'You think it was *funny*?' he demanded thunderously.

'Not it. You,' said Seven, enjoying his discomposure when before he had been so *certain*, the master lover...

'Really? And who are you to judge?' he snarled cuttingly. 'A virgin who didn't even know what she was doing half the time? Let me tell you, lady, that whatever problems may have attended my previous relationships I've never had any complaints about my performance in bed.'

Strangely, Seven wasn't offended, or even jealous, at his crudely cocky jibe. 'Of course not, you're *very* very good,' she told him with just the right touch of condescension. It was a marvellous feeling, to lie flagrantly naked with a man and infuriate him, she decided. She, who didn't even know how to flirt! 'It's just that...' She hesitated tantalisingly, pursing her mouth primly.

'Just what?' His eyes were sultry black, his mouth a sullen slash, the velvet sandpaper which covered the lower half of his unshaven face, and which he had used so inventively, to such shattering effect, in his lovemaking, all added to the air of virile, smouldering temper that hovered over his side of the bed.

'Just...well... I like my men to be a little more, well...self-confident and sure of themselves——'

'*Men?*' he exploded, vibrating with outrage. Then it hit him: his shy little ex-virgin was mocking him. Her grey eyes were dancing with tiny lavender sparks, her lovely breasts quivering with the effort of withheld mirth, the soft rose nipples taunting him with their tumescence. Why, the teasing witch was amused by his doubt, was playing on it shamelessly, was even a little aroused by her wicked daring. Hot relief flooded into his chest and loins, tightening them with a renewed thrust of passion and pride. He *hadn't* frightened her with the violence of his lovemaking. She was his. She *liked* him big and bold and hungry. He didn't *have* to hold anything back for fear of hurting her...

He growled and pounced, squashing out of her in a rush the laughter she had been valiantly repressing. 'I'm sorry, I'm sorry...' She giggled without remorse as he stormed deliciously over her. 'But I thought I was getting a man...not a beardless boy...'

'Beardless...?' He scraped the evidence to the contrary across the tender peaks of her breasts, and when her laughter turned to sighs he drew her hand to the other, irrefutable evidence of his manhood, showing her how to touch him, how to share the pleasure. 'Ah, Seven, you feel so good...' He kissed her ripe mouth. 'Do you know how I fought this? And all because I have a hang-up about small, helpless women who arouse my battered protective instincts. But you arouse more than just my protective instincts—just to look at you is to want you, even though I kept telling myself that you weren't my type.' He pushed himself up on braced arms, sealing the centres of their bodies, and looked down at her with all the delight of his discovery in his eyes. 'But I was wrong about you, wasn't I? I don't have to worry about you because it's not my protection you *want*. You may be small but you're strong, and you may be shy but you're not helpless...sometimes you make *me* feel weak...'

'Don't worry, I'll protect you,' Seven whispered, stroking her hand over that hard, beloved jaw, drawing him down to her. There was a faint flicker of shock in the black eyes and she suddenly knew that no one had ever made that offer before, even in jest. Jake had always been the strong one, the one that other people leaned on, the invincible, turning defeat into triumph, tragedy into usable copy.

This time it was long and slow and easy, made even more intensely erotic by the daylight that flooded in the window, washing them with its cold, revealing glare so that not the faintest response to word or kiss or caress escaped unremarked. There was something awfully decadent, Seven thought, sighing blissfully, about making love in the morning...

'Oh, yes, you're the Queen of Decadence,' Jake murmured in lazy amusement when she said as much. 'You're well on the slippery slope to depravity...'

'I hope so.' She delighted him with her demure grin. Even naked and well-loved, she still retained an essential purity that had nothing to do with her physical state. It was as if there was part of her that was untouchable, inviolate, where not even a lover could reach. She who had originally appeared so open and transparent had proved instead to be a mystery, wrapped in an enigma, and only now was he beginning to appreciate the true implications of inviting her into his life...

They lay peacefully entwined, skirting the edge of sleep, each absorbed in lazy, pleasurable dreams, until the intimate isolation was shattered by the persistent, echoing call of the telephone from the empty hall.

Ten minutes later they were on their way to Auckland Hospital, Seven still buttoning her blouse under her cardigan and struggling with a pair of tights Jake had refused to wait for her to don. Charlotte Jackson had had a heart attack and for once Aunt Jane hadn't dithered. She had called an ambulance and travelled with it, phoning Seven from the emergency department waiting-room.

Seven looked across to the tight-lipped man at the wheel of the powerful car. Grey, tense, haggard, he was a far cry from the laughing, languorous lover of only a few minutes ago. She wondered briefly if that man was gone forever.

'Jake——' She wanted to reassure him, but hadn't the words. Wanted reassurance herself, but didn't know what to ask for.

He flicked her a glance as he slammed the gears through a rapid change, cursing as he ran a red light.

'Not now. Later.' Then with grim perspicacity he added, 'But if you're feeling guilty, mouse, at what we were doing while Mother was having her attack, don't. Our making love wasn't a sin that brought swift retribution, it was an affirmation of life—yours and mine.'

His use of that affectionate, annoying nickname quietened her more effectively than the rest of his words. He used it deliberately, as a statement of intent, of possession. And she was with him at a time of crisis, a time when people gathered around them the things that they needed...loved...

CHAPTER NINE

THE heart attack was not as severe as the doctors at first thought, but Charlotte remained for several days in Intensive Care before being moved to a convalescent ward.

Seven knew it was her fault; Charlotte had found another of Seven's sketches, a portrait of Rebecca. But this wasn't the baby Becky from the photographs that adorned the walls and albums, it was an older Becky, a wistful Becky with no laughter in her eyes, a thin and wasted Becky. Seven hadn't liked it when she had done it, quickly, feverishly, trying to drive the image out of her head, but neither had she been able to destroy the ugly portrait. Here I am, said the picture. I'm waiting. Why don't you come and get me? It was an accusation, a reproach.

Seven hadn't been able to destroy it, but Jake had. When Aunt Jane had falteringly admitted, during the first anxious hour of waiting at the hospital, that she had found Charlotte's unconscious body with the sketch clutched in her hand, he had glanced at it coldly, but there had been no coldness in the way he had ripped it into confetti and flung it into the hospital rubbish bin. Yet he had not uttered one word of condemnation, which to a guilt-racked Seven had been a condemnation in itself. When, after he had finally seen Charlotte, conscious but disorientated, and heard the doctor's verdict that, considering the damaged state of her heart, another attack was very possible, Seven had tried to force an anguished apology on him. His response had been steely.

'Oh, no, Seven, you're not going to use guilt to withdraw from me. You're not getting away from me that easily...'

In the next breath he was ordering them out of his life. 'I think it would be best if you move back into your own home,' he told them flatly. 'At this point Mother is my first priority. Everything else will have to wait until she gets well...'

Aunt Jane accepted the suggestion with uncharacteristic meekness, satisfied by the hint that her current hot 'case' was only being temporarily shelved. She had plenty of other, smaller fish to fry in the meantime. To Seven, his casual dismissal confirmed her deepest fears. In spite of his words he was pushing her away. His desire for her had only been a transient impulse, not deeply rooted enough to survive the first storm. But how could it be otherwise? She blamed herself... why shouldn't he?

'Dammit, Seven, don't look at me like that. We can't change what happened——'

'I know—Charlotte—it's my fault. If she hadn't found that picture——' She looked down at her white knuckles, her eyes blurring with tears that refused to fall.

'It would have been something else,' he said curtly. 'We've been half expecting something like this. It's her heart that's at fault, not you. You didn't cause her disease.'

He was being kind. She couldn't bear it! She would rather have his anger. 'But I knew about it. You told me that she wasn't in good health and I thought it was just an excuse to try and get rid of Aunt Jane and me——'

'And you think this is another excuse?' He finally divined the exact source of her distress. He pulled her away from her aunt. 'Seven, don't let that wild imagination of yours run away with you. I'm not asking you to leave because I want you gone.' His mouth curved in gentle self-derision. 'Quite to the reverse. I want you too *much*.

I can't live with you and not have you in my bed. It
would drive me crazy. And somehow I don't think you'd
be comfortable with that. I can't imagine you creeping
along to my bedroom every night, worrying whether your
aunt is going to wake up and what she might hear or
see, and if I suddenly moved you into a room of your
own she'd want to know why.' He raised his eyebrow
and she blushed. In some ways he knew her too well; it
was almost demeaning.

'I never wanted to come and live with you in the first
place,' she reminded him proudly.

He took her cold hand in his, his voice softly threat-
ening. 'Don't get in a snit, mouse. This is for *your* sake,
not for mine. Personally, I don't give a damn who knows
we're lovers. You can't put the clock back, Seven, and
I'm not going to let your conscience turn me into your
first experience of a one-night stand. Clandestine or not,
we *are* lovers, and at least this way we'll have some
privacy. I have a pretty rough schedule, and with Mother
ill it'll be worse, but I want us to be together as often
as we can.'

As it happened that wasn't very often over the next
week. A snatched hour here and there, and all of them,
to their mutual frustration, in public places—res-
taurants, the hospital cafeteria or waiting-room...the
library. Never once did they make it back to the avowed
privacy of his house. Once again Seven was brought face
to face with the effect of extreme pressures upon Jake.
He became almost incandescent with energy and, denied
the pressure-valve of physical release, it manifested itself
in even more vitriolic than usual editorials and a moody,
unpredictable temper. He was either furiously lo-
quacious, exploding with words and ideas, or curt and
taciturn and murderously succinct. Seven was fascinated. With her it was always words, as if by talking he
could stop himself reaching across the restaurant table
and tearing her clothes off. Because that was what her

tingling senses told her he wanted to do. He confirmed it with his smouldering eyes, with his constant touching. It was headily reassuring. Once she had met him at the offices of the *Clarion* at his request, before going out to the nearby restaurant for dinner, and going down in the lift he had thrust her against the wall and taken her mouth with a raging appetite that she had ached to appease.

'Let's not go and eat,' he growled, shuddering at her quick response, his hands cupping her breasts through the lacy ruffles of her blouse, his hips grinding her against the padded wall. 'Let's go back upstairs to my office and lock the door...'

For an instant, Seven actually entertained the possibility. 'But your office has glass walls,' she pointed out huskily. And it was in the centre of the big newsroom.

'I'll call a fire drill and get rid of everybody.'

'And what about tomorrow's paper...?' she teased him about his precious priority.

'To hell with the first edition!' he compromised, taking even greater liberties with her person. The lift gave a slight jolt and the doors slid open on the ground floor. Two men, one armed with a camera, looked on with interest.

'What the hell are you staring at, Potter?' Jake snarled at the photographer.

'Just wondering whether it's worth a shot for the notice-board, J.J.,' the man said jauntily.

'You try,' Jake invited savagely. 'And I'll shove that camera so far down your throat that when you——'

'Jake——!' Seven finished smoothing down her skirt and pleaded with him not to over-react.

'Just joking, J.J.' Potter grinned unrepentantly, and his companion snickered at the alliteration.

'I think it's called getting a taste of your own medicine,' murmured Seven sweetly, recalling some of the intrusive celebrity photographs she had seen in the *Clarion*. Jake glowered at her.

'You can afford to be snide,' he said sarcastically. 'I suppose you don't care that it's your half-exposed bosom that would occupy the better part of the frame.'

Seven looked down to discover that he had flicked open some buttons during their brief but torrid embrace, and clutched the edges of her blouse together with a vivid blush.

'Going to introduce us, Chief?' asked the other man, encouraged by the by-play.

'Get lost!' Jake elbowed past the mirthful pair.

'You do know her name, don't you?' the irreverent Potter shouted after them. 'Or did you two just meet in the lift? Hey, J.J., where're ya going? We just want the intimate details . . . off the record and all that!'

'No comment,' Seven managed to call back as she was hustled out of the revolving glass door of the building.

'Give you a little confidence and you go mad,' he said sourly, as they ducked through a sudden shower to the restaurant. 'You should have let me handle it. Those two will make my life a misery.'

'You started it,' said Seven virtuously. 'All they did was smile and you jumped down their throats.'

'I didn't like the way they were looking at you, or what they were thinking. That Potter has a mind like a sewer.'

'I thought that was a prerequisite for working on your paper,' said Seven, opening her menu, only to have it snatched from her hand. She met his frustrated temper with a cool excitement, knowing its source. 'After all, he was right, wasn't he? If the lift had taken longer we'd have been . . . been . . .' Her teasing courage faded and she began to blush as his annoyance turned into amusement.

'Come on, don't stop there, mouse,' he taunted softly. 'Where's all that heady confidence now? I'm interested to know how far you would have gone with me. All the way? In a lift? Is that what you wanted?'

'Certainly not!' she said breathlessly, blushing more deeply as he chuckled. 'Can we order now? I'm hungry.'

'So am I, mouse,' he murmured as he handed back her menu to screen her hot cheeks. 'So am I. But don't worry. The time will come when we'll be able to gorge ourselves to our hearts' content...'

But her heart could never be content, not loving a man like Jake Jackson—the passionate cynic whose everyday work confirmed his cynicism. For there was no future in it. He wanted her as a lover, but if she offered the totality of her love she knew he would reject it and she would lose him. Love he bitterly equated with the nightmare consequences of helplessness, so Jake wanted only strength in his relationships.

Then there was her 'gift', the one he professed to understand, if not actually believe—that too was a barrier. On the second day of Charlotte's stay in Intensive Care, Jake had become enraged by the specialist's understanding cautious refusal to speculate on her chances of recovery at such an early stage. Jake wanted the facts, but the facts in this case were obscured by the intangible variables of medical science—the patient's will to live, her uniquely individual reaction to treatment, her state of general health....

Jake had been bitingly rude, and in the middle of the heated discussion had electrified the specialist and the intern who had been also been present by turning abruptly on Seven.

'Well, if they won't tell me, maybe you will. Is my mother going to live?'

'I...I don't know,' she stammered, startled by the apparent attack.

'Oh, come on, Seven,' he sneered. 'Your "science" appears to be just as exact as theirs! What does her aura look like?'

Seven knew she was being used as a combination whipping-boy and goad, but understanding didn't make it easier to bear.

'I have no idea,' she said as calmly as she could. 'Excuse me...I need some air.'

He had come after her and taken her in his arms and, as usual, persuaded her to forgive him, but under her wan smile a knot of uneasiness tightened into painful certainty. His scepticism denied an essential part of her that was indivisible from the whole. Could a cynical, down-to-earth, pragmatic man like Jake ever truly be comfortable with the dark, inexplicable 'other-worldliness' that sometimes controlled her? What right did she have to demand someone else to share the weari-some burden she had been born with...especially someone that she loved and who might be hurt by it? And she feared that Jake would be hurt...for Seven had found the source of her nightmares.

That first day when they had rushed to the hospital Seven had dismissed her faint sensation of nausea as worry about Charlotte. But each time she had visited the hospital, she had felt worse. On the day that a much improved Charlotte had been transferred out of Intensive Care, Seven had got lost trying to find her new ward. The habitual tension that was a constant companion turned into a case of full-blown panic when she had turned a sharp corner and found herself looking down a long, white, empty corridor. The strip lighting overhead had been cold and bright. The doors at the far end had been green. Recognition had been instant. As in her dream Seven had stood rooted to the spot until a passing orderly had stopped to ask if she was all right. Seven had nodded sickly and asked where the nearest public toilets were. Once there she had been gratefully ill.

She was very careful not to get lost again, but the dangerous knowledge was now there, inside her, building relentlessly. She had been too caught up in panic to notice any signs, so she didn't know what awaited her behind those doors, but she knew that she would have no peace until she found out.

The fearful reluctance was at least as great as the mental compulsion, and it took her days to overcome it. One evening she arrived early for visiting, accompanied by Aunt Jane as usual, and, after dropping her aunt off at the administration block, slowly retraced her steps through the maze of corridors. Her feet seemed to remember the way, even if her mind refused to admit it. When she took the last turning she saw the sign. And then she *knew*...

Children's Ward.

The nurse wouldn't let her go in. Even during visiting hours, she said, which were staggered, only parents and approved visitors were allowed.

In a daze Seven made her way back to Charlotte's room and collapsed into the bedside chair.

'Good heavens, you look terrible, Seven!' the older woman cried. 'Are you ill? Is it Jane?'

Her anxiety jolted Seven out of her shocked abstraction. The doctors, not to mention Jake, would be furious if she upset Charlotte. The older woman was still shaky, although she had recovered enough to undertake some mild therapy and complain about her new diet and the fact that she was having to give up smoking—endure 'cold turkey'. Jake! He would know what to do!

'No—no Aunt Jane is fine. In fact she's gone down to the office to volunteer as an official hospital visitor...' Her aunt had discovered a rich vein of potential clients in the captive wards of bored patients. 'W...where's Jake, is he coming?'

'He said he would if he could, you know what Jake's like. Did you see the flowers he sent...?'

Seven listened but didn't hear. She sat in a claustrophobic haze, unaware of Charlotte's increasingly sharp looks. At last there was a familiarly impatient shove on the swing door of the small private room and Jake was there. He kissed his mother and she whispered something in his ear. He turned and supported Seven by the elbow as she rose shakily from her chair.

'Seven?' He put a hand to her bleached cheek and felt the clamminess, saw the violet turmoil in her eyes.

'I . . . need to talk to you,' she said, casting a sidelong look at Charlotte, and thankfully Jake took the hint. With a word to his mother he drew Seven gently out into the corridor.

'What is it, mouse? Are you ill?' He took a sharp breath and the question came out of nowhere. 'Are you *pregnant*?'

He didn't know what made him ask, particularly since it had only been just over ten days since they had made love. Even if she were pregnant the baby would hardly exist yet, and certainly it was too soon for her to experience any signs. It wasn't until days later that he'd realised that he had taken no precautions that first night, and even though Seven had assured him that it was a safe period for her he had been shocked at his appalling act of carelessness. But somehow the idea that had once filled him with horror seemed no longer such a terrifying prospect. In fact . . .

Seven stared at him, too panicked by his unexpected question to notice his remarkable lack of answering panic. 'I don't know . . . No . . . no, I can't be,' she dismissed frantically. 'Not the first time . . . besides, it was safe!'

'Once is all it takes,' he reminded her softly. 'And "safe" is relative.'

She knew what he was thinking. 'It wasn't deliberate, Jake, I *swear* . . .' He caught her cold, fluttering hands and drew them warmly against his chest.

'I know . . . I know. Calm down, darling. Don't you think I realise that there's a world of difference between you and a woman like Chloe? If you *are* pregnant it should be me who begs forgiveness—I was the more experienced of the two of us, I should have kept my head. Instead I just threw myself on you like a randy, brainless kid.' His heart beat steadily, strongly, into her hands as his voice deepened. 'It's not the end of the world if it happens. We're both mature enough to cope. But let's not cross that bridge until we come to it. I'm sorry for even worrying you about it, when you're so obviously already badly upset about something else. What is it? Talk to me, Seven...'

So she talked. She told him about the dream that night that had driven her to Rebecca's room. She told him about her feelings, the strange compulsion that had drawn her to the children's ward. She told him what it meant.

'She's there, Jake. Rebecca's there. She's ill. I know she is. Don't ask me how or why. I just *know*...'

She could see in his navy eyes the rejection, and the same craving that had eaten at her. The desire for knowledge almost perfectly balanced by the fear what that knowledge would be.

'Are you sure?' The words were torn laboriously from his throat. 'Have you seen her?'

'The nurse wouldn't let me in.'

It wasn't the same nurse, but she wouldn't have let them in, either, if it weren't for Jake flashing his Press card and using all of his brutal charm to persuade her that his newspaper wanted to open an appeal to provide extra funds for the children's ward at a time when hospitals were paring back on their budgets.

'Naturally nothing will be published without full consultation with the hospital administration. Perhaps I could get permission to interview you and some of your colleagues...?'

Seven was shivering violently by the time they were eagerly ushered into the first light, airy, colourful room lined with beds. Eight children to a room, the nurse had said, and four rooms, plus several doubles and singles for those who required special treatment, or who were infectious. Even as his eyes rapidly skimmed the beds Jake was taking off his suit jacket and draping it around Seven's narrow shoulders in an absent gesture of possessive concern. She was instantly comforted by the residual warmth from his body, the familiar musky, male fragrance that soothed her raw senses.

'Not here,' Seven whispered, and they moved on, past the stares of those children who were well enough to be curious. The deeper they went into the ward, the greyer and more controlled Jake became, and when Seven slipped her hand into his he gripped it with unconscious cruelty. The next few minutes were every bit as long as the previous six years.

She was in the end bed in the third room. The favoured window-bed that was usually claimed by the longest resident. She was breakably thin, translucently pale, but her eyes were a luminous blue, cornflower-blue. The girl from the sketch. Rebecca. And around her neck, above the pretty sprigged nightie, she wore a worn gold, heart-shaped locket. Jake's palm was suddenly slick with sweat, his expression a combination of agony, relief, and sheer terror. He was looking at the lost part of himself. His heart, his soul, his joy. His throat worked but he couldn't utter a word, so it was left to Seven to say tentatively,

'Rebecca?'

The little girl looked up from the book she was buried in, tucking her fine, straight, dark blonde hair behind her small ears.

'Hi. That's me. Are you a new doctor? Oh, no, you can't be, you haven't got a white coat. Why do they always have to be white, I wonder? It would be much more cheerful if they were coloured, don't you think? Or many-coloured, like Joseph's. Have you seen that musical about the Dreamcoat? That's one of my favourites.' A big, sunny smile that matched the natural eagerness of her voice, and no pause for breath, or an answer. 'Are you visiting someone? It's not visiting time, yet—did you sneak in? Sister Kay will chase you out, you know, she hates anyone trying to wreck her routine . . .'

Seven shook her head in bemusement at the bright chatter from the little wraith on the bed.

'I talk too much,' grinned the girl, reading her mind. 'I know. Mum and Dad are always telling me to *listen* but I have so much to *say*. And if I don't say it how are people going to know what it is? You're very fair, are you Swedish——?'

'Your parents. Are they coming today?' Jake interrupted, his demand so bitterly harsh the girl's bright face faded in puzzlement.

'It isn't visiting time yet,' she repeated, uncertainly, and Seven gave Jake's hot, damp hand a warning squeeze.

'I'm a New Zealander, but my mother's parents were Swiss—I suppose that's where I get my colouring.' Seven drew Rebecca's attention back to herself. 'Sometimes I don't feel that I came from anywhere because I never remember one place as home, we were always travelling. My parents were circus people.'

'Really? How fantastic!' The ready smile appeared again, highlighting the gauntness of the small face. 'I'm going to be a dancer when I grow up. Not ballet, that's too, you know, *restricting*.' She looked smug at the impressive word. 'I want to do lots of different kinds of dancing. Are you in the circus, too?'

Seven talked comfortably for a while, holding the fort until she felt Jake relax his tortured stiffness and begin to shift restlessly, aching for his share of attention. His first tentative remark was received with polite caution, but soon his genuine fascination with Rebecca was working as well as his practised lies had on the charge

nurse. Tucked inside his jacket, Seven perched on the
radiator by the window-ledge, while Jake, with a rude
comment about hospital rules that made Rebecca bubble
with laughter, sat on the end of her bed.

She had been admitted to hospital with meningitis,
but she was getting better now. In fact she was due to
leave the next week. Seven and Jake exchanged looks of
chilled horror and relief as Rebecca went on to proudly
inform them that everyone had thought she was going
to die, except her. She knew God didn't want her to die
yet, not before he had given her a chance to dance.

In her aimless, happy chatter she told them that her
father's name was Alec Hastings and he was a teacher,
and that they had come to New Zealand direct from the
Australian outback only a few weeks ago. 'Dad's a Kiwi,
you see, and he wants us to go to school here. He says
this is where his roots are. He wants Micky—that's my
brother—to go to the same school he did.' And then the
artless admission that shattered Jake's composure all over
again. 'Of course Micky's not my *real* brother—I'm
adopted, you know. Mum and Dad adopted me when
they thought they couldn't have children, but then Micky
came along. Micky's only four and I'm eight, and he's
a pest sometimes, but Mum said that I was, too, when
I was four, only I had no one to pester but her and Dad.
I was stuck in here for my birthday, but Mum says she's
going to have a big party for me when I get out...'

'I...how old were you when your parents adopted
you?' prompted Jake huskily, incredibly grateful to his
daughter for being such a chatterbox. For she was his
daughter, there was not an atom of doubt left in his
reeling mind.

'Nearly three. I don't know about my real dad, but
my real mother wasn't very old and she couldn't afford
to keep me. She left me this locket—see—it's got my
name on it, *Rebecca*, that's the only thing she had. She
travelled around a lot and I guess it was hard for her

with a baby an' all. My mum says that I should feel sorry for her because she had the gift of life and she gave it up, but I don't know. I think people who have babies should keep them, don't you? I mean, it's not like a toy or anything that you can get another one the same. But then if my real mum hadn't given me away I wouldn't have my mum and dad, and Micky, and we're a *proper* family. That's a picture of us all on Micky's birthday...'

Seven rose to look over Jake's shoulder at the photograph Rebecca had proudly produced out of the bedside drawer. Mr and Mrs Hastings were fair, like Rebecca, and so was their chubby son. Their eyes were all tinted red by the flash, which added to the likeness, and they all looked happy. A nice, ordinary family out for a celebration.

'A proper family,' murmured Jake, running his thumb over his daughter's merry image. Seven heard the utter desolation of loss in his voice. Whatever had happened in the past, whatever horror the baby Rebecca had endured, as a young girl she had risen magnificently above it. She was a bright, intelligent, lively and outgoing girl that anyone would be proud to have as a daughter. She loved and was loved in return. From her artless chatter it appeared that she wanted for nothing. Especially not a father. Her speech was peppered with 'Mum said' and 'Dad said', and she patently adored her 'pest' of a brother.

Even so, Jake couldn't bring himself to leave. In the half an hour before visiting time officially began he greedily drank in the sight and sound of Rebecca Hastings, and when the signal bell rang he had to clench his fists in order not to reach out and take what was his, take the love and affection that should have been his due. To give her all of his. But he knew that it would only frighten and wound her—his lovely, miracle child who was now someone else's miracle.

He wanted to scream and rage and kidnap her as she had once been kidnapped from him. Instead he smiled, and waggled his fingers in a casual goodbye, and took the arm of a miracle that *was* his to claim, and left.

CHAPTER TEN

SEVEN poked sourly at the log on the reluctant fire. She had put it on too soon, before the kindling was properly alight. Now it was smoking sullenly, and if she wanted more kindling she would have to go out in the rain and get it from the stack in the courtyard. Impatience had never been one of her problems before. She had always decided what she wanted first, then steadily, meticulously, gone the right way about getting it—acceptance at school, good marks, her librarian's diploma. Yes, everything had always turned out for the best, thanks to her ability to work quietly and steadily towards her goals. Striving for something you wanted was very fulfilling, but she was now discovering how much harder it was *not* to strive for something that you wanted above all else.

That was the reason she was alone now, in a tatty little rented cabin in an empty beach resort, with a stack of books she wouldn't need. The lure of the imaginative world of fiction was no longer irresistible, thanks to Jake. He had coloured reality too vividly for her to settle any longer for shadows. She loved him, but there wasn't a place for her in his life. It was the cruellest lesson she had ever had to learn, and this unplanned little holiday in the miserable depths of winter was supposed to help her accept it. She was having as much success with that as she was with the fire in the hearth. One day in her self-imposed wilderness and she was going stir-crazy!

Aunt Jane had said she was mad to rush off without telling anyone where she was going, or why. She had demanded to know what Seven was trying to achieve and, when that didn't elicit any answers, pronounced darkly that she would regret it, that her stars were all wrong for solitude.

Seven hated to admit it but Aunt Jane had been partly right. What was the point in being bad-tempered and cynical and disillusioned by shattered hopes when there was nobody around to commiserate, or take it out on? The only person Seven had to fight with was herself, and it was a losing battle.

Of course she had been right to disentangle herself from Jake's life, she told herself for the hundredth time, as she marched through to the tiny kitchen of the three-room cabin and tried to get interested in the pot of soup she had reheated for the second time. Jake was going through hell at the moment because of her. Inevitably his bitter, underlying resentment would tear them apart anyway. Why hang around begging for heartbreak? Why not just get it over with? Act decisively.

Jake had been decisive. He had not spoken to the Hastingses that first time. He had been grimly determined that when he did it would be in full command of his emotions and in full possession of all the facts. With the names, dates and places that Rebecca had unknowingly provided the rest had been relatively easy. From various sources Jake had been able, within a few days, to loosely piece together the events of six years ago, after the couple from the Auckland boarding house, Sharon Riley and Keith Smythe, had taken their "deceased" daughter to Australia.

Jessica and Alec Hastings had adopted that baby—Rebecca—by private arrangement, in the remote Australian mining township where Alec had been teaching at the time. Sharon Riley, who had been living hand-to-mouth on welfare payments, had stayed with the couple for nearly six months after Jessica had gen-

erously taken pity on her plight. Sharon had told them
that her toddler's father, her *de facto* husband, had been
killed in a car accident, shortly after they had arrived
in Western Australia. They had been travelling through
remote stretches of the country, undoubtedly avoiding
big towns and cities, Keith working at labouring jobs
wherever he could find them. After he was killed, Sharon
had continued, aimlessly moving from place to place,
finding her child more and more of a burden as she
struggled to survive. When the Hastingses had taken her
in she had been at the end of her tether, but during the
next few months she had bounced back, even finding a
job as a check-out operator at the company store and
leaving her 'daughter' more and more in Jessica's care
as she rediscovered the pleasures of being young and free
and single. She had distanced herself increasingly from
Rebecca as Jessica took over her mothering, and eventually had offered to sign a paper handing over legal
guardianship to the then childless couple. Friends of the
Hastingses remembered that Sharon Riley had seemed
to genuinely care for her daughter and yet at the same
time resent her. It had been well known how badly the
Hastingses wanted a child of their own, and no one had
been particularly surprised how things turned out.
Sharon had been a pretty girl, if a bit nervy and high-
strung, but she had still been, at twenty, little more than
a child herself, and her increasingly irresponsible
behaviour had raised eyebrows but no ire. She had left
in the company of a young engineer, and although she
had shed a few public tears when she had said farewell
to her daughter the consensus had been that the tears
were as much relief as sadness, and that she was doing
the right thing by the child—giving Becky the chance of
a settled life with two parents who loved and wanted her,
rather than the insecurity of a transient lifestyle with a

mother who was enjoying her new-found freedom too much to want to be tied down.

Jake, when he read the reports, saw it somewhat differently, as did the psychologist he consulted. Guilt had probably been the guiding factor in Sharon's action. During the first few months, the 'honeymoon period' as the psychologist had called it, Sharon had probably been able to convince herself that Rebecca truly was hers. But gradually the secret knowledge would have eaten its way to the surface, and she would have begun to confront the reality that no substitute was going to be able to replace her feelings for her lost baby. Duncan Hedges was of the opinion that Sharon herself had snatched Rebecca, and that Keith Smythe had gone along with it just for the sake of appeasing her. By all accounts their relationship had sharply deteriorated in Australia, and they had been on the verge of splitting up when he was killed, so perhaps his resentment at taking on the burden of someone else's child had contributed to Sharon's disillusionment. But speculations about Sharon's state of mind would have to remain just that—speculation. For she, too, was now dead, ironically in the same way as her baby, by drowning—while she was swimming at a treacherous east coast surf beach.

That left Jake with nothing. Nobody to vent his rage on, nobody to wreak vengeance upon, to pay as he'd sworn somebody would, for their crime. Even the evidence that Sharon had, in her way, taken scrupulous care of his daughter conspired to thwart him. A fierce, unadulterated hatred would have been infinitely more satisfying than the remorseless sense of pity that he was left with. He was horrified to share with his tormentor the intimate knowledge of supreme grief that the loss of a child brought. A grief that could so easily tip over into a kind of temporary insanity.

Seven's love had been at its strongest as Jake had raged violently through his emotional storms. She had listened while he tortured himself with options that they both knew weren't really options at all. She had gone with him when he endured the daily agony of casually dropping in to see a once-and-future daughter whom he dared not frighten with his feelings. She had held him in the depths of the night when he was pursued by demons.

For the entire week that Rebecca had remained in hospital he had existed in a kind of limbo. It was only on the day she was due to go home, when he had the final proof in his hand—a set of Rebecca Hastings' X-rays with the betraying bone formation clearly matching the other, older set—that he had forced himself to confront her adoptive parents. They had been as shattered and grief-stricken as he. And they had had guilt of their own to cope with.

'We suspected that the adoption might not be entirely legal—I guess that's why we never formally registered the change in surname,' a distraught Jessica Hastings had sobbed. 'But we had no idea that she wasn't Sharon's daughter. As far as we were concerned she was Rebecca Riley, she still is. You can't take her away. Not after all this time. You can't take my baby! Alec, you're not going to let him, are you? There must be something we can do. Becky is *ours*!'

Her husband had tried to be supportive, but it was obvious that he, too, was panicked at the idea that this big, dark stranger had the legal right to walk into their lives and take their beloved daughter, just when they were getting over the shock of her life-threatening illness. His thin face had been ashen, his eyes bewildered behind his spectacles as he'd held his wife's trembling figure and said in a cracked voice: 'Now, Jess, there's no need for hysterics. I'm sure that Mr Jackson isn't going to rush into anything. He knows we love Becky.' His dark brown eyes had burned into Jake's rigid stare. 'Come on, love, you don't want to frighten Micky. We've got to be strong for his sake, and for Becky's. We've got to discuss this reasonably.'

With each word it seemed that his voice had strengthened with determination. The two men, father to the same child, had been locked into a silent challenge as they had stared at each other and Duncan Hedges, who had insisted on being present, had tensed himself for trouble. But Jake had risen magnificently to the occasion. In a quiet, controlled speech that had torn at Seven's heart, he had told the Hastings that he wasn't going to fight them for custody, providing they didn't object to Becky's being told that Jake was her real father. He wanted reasonable access for himself and his mother, and to establish a trust fund to be used at the Hastingses' discretion for Becky's education, health and welfare.

'I think that, at least, is my right—to make sure that my daughter doesn't suffer for not legally being my daughter. In exchange I'm prepared to support the legalisation of the adoption. There'll be no problem getting her mother's agreement, I can assure you of that. I only hope that it won't cause Becky any problems in the future to learn that her father and mother weren't married, or that Chloe never really wanted a child.'

'That's her loss, not Becky's,' Jessica Hastings had choked, her tears shining like jewels in her pathetically grateful eyes. 'I think you'll find that Becky will be more curious than upset,' she'd been eager to convince him. 'She has a great imagination and interest in everything that goes on, and a loving generosity of spirit that if anything is *too* forgiving...'

'I know,' Jake had said quietly. 'You can be very proud of your daughter.'

'And you of yours,' Alec Hastings had added. The two men had shaken hands in grim understanding of the nature of their armed truce. Seven had envied them their trust. Hers had been fast draining away. Jake had condemned himself to hover on the sidelines of Rebecca's life, to exist on the left-overs of her affection. Could he ever look at Seven and not remember the agonising decision she had forced upon him, not wonder what other bizarre torments that her 'gift' might cause in the future, to him, and to those he loved?

With masochistic clarity Seven recalled the last time they had made love. It had been in his queen-sized bed, in the early evening just before he'd left to pick up his mother, an ecstatic born-again grandmother, on her discharge from the hospital. In the heat of the moment the forbidden words had escaped her. As she'd reached her peak she had cried out that she loved him. And his answer? A heavy silence, followed by a smothering of kisses that had thrust the trembling confession back down her throat. He didn't want to know how she felt. He didn't want her love, and she couldn't add to his hurts by forcing him to hurt her. When he had left, so had she. The next morning she had rung the council claiming a family bereavement, telling her supervisor that she was taking the week's holiday that was owing. If it hadn't been granted she would have gone anyway. Her career was the last thing on her mind.

Seven left the soup congealing unappetisingly in the saucepan and wandered miserably back into the lounge. The amount of smoke was now quite alarming so she doused the feeble fire with water, but that only made the problem worse. Hurriedly she ran over and threw the door wide open—and gave a screech of terror. A shadowy figure was standing there. Visions from *Psycho* danced in her head—the same ones that ensured she hadn't slept a wink last night.

'For God's sake, what are you trying to do, woman? Commit suttee?' Jake barked. Ignoring her spluttering protests, he pushed past her and went over to the fire-place, snorting when he saw the mess. He pulled the damp log off with the fire-tongs and reached over to a stack of yellowing newspapers, piled in the wood-basket. Slowly, methodically, he rolled up a series of tight tubes and arranged them in the grate with loosely crumpled paper beneath. The only time he looked or spoke, to Seven's stunned shock, it was to say curtly, 'Why don't you shut the damned door? Unless you want to add flood to our problems.'

The steady rain was driving in over the doorstep. Seven obeyed numbly and then stood, not really believing her eyes, as Jake got the fire going with arrogant ease. At last he stood up, dusting his hands on his dark trousers. He was wearing a suit, which looked incongruous in the present surroundings, and Seven swallowed. Jake never wore a suit in his spare time, he preferred casual clothes, so it was a safe assumption that when he had left Auckland it had been in too much of a hurry to change.

He was in no hurry now. He was letting her sweat. He stood, hands on hips, inspecting her from the tips of her slippers up over the ubiquitous plain skirt and blouse topped by a rather smart navy cardigan-jacket, to her huge-eyed, apprehensive face. She looked more like a guilty schoolgirl than a runaway lover. He very nearly smiled, but he refused to give her the advantage of knowing that his anger was mostly bluff.

'Well?' he demanded, with all the arrogance he could summon. Sure enough her chin jolted up and those shock-glazed eyes began to smoulder.

'As I recall, suttee was preformed by *wives*,' she snapped back, chosing to answer his initial goad, which had rankled.

His eyebrows rose. 'And favoured concubines, so I believe.'

Seven blanched at the cruel blow, then flushed with renewed fury. 'Well, I'm neither. And I wouldn't throw myself on a *your* pyre for all the tea in China!'

'Not much of a bargain,' he agreed. 'How about, for all my worldly goods?'

She choked on a gasp, and he laughed, unforgivably. 'I wouldn't marry you if you begged me!' she spat venomously.

'Pity. All that love going to waste.'

Pity! She felt sick and faint at the same time. He felt responsible for seducing her and making her fall in love with him when all he had wanted was an affair. He had come to relieve his conscience.

'How did you find me? Did Aunt Jane tell you?'

'How could she? She didn't know. Nor did your replacement at the library, nor any of your assistants. Nor did any of your friends. Tina Tracey was right, you're a secretive little thing, aren't you?'

'You mean you went around *asking* people? How dare you interfere in my private affairs?'

It was a rotten choice of words. 'I *am* your private affair,' he pointed out. 'Have you got anything to eat here? I'm starved. I haven't eaten since breakfast. I had a paper to put out as well as running around trying to find you.'

'Nobody asked you to,' she told him, her stomach heaving at the thought of food. 'Didn't the fact that I didn't tell anyone where I was going give you a tiny *hint* that I mightn't want to be found?'

Her sarcasm bounced off the back of his head. She followed him out into the kitchen where he looked with disapproval at the turgid soup. He opened the wheezing fridge and discovered milk and eggs and butter.

'Is this all you've got? You are wallowing in self-pity, aren't you?' said Jake, taking them out and putting them on the bench as he searched the ill-equipped cutlery drawer. 'Omelette OK?'

If he hadn't taken down the frying-pan for himself, Seven would have brained him with it.

'Self-pity?' she raged. 'I thought you were the one with the monopoly on that! You let one tragedy twist your whole life out of proportion! You lost the one you loved so you were never going to love again. Well, you can find someone else to be your mistress. Eventually I'm sure you'll find a woman who's happy just to be your emotionless sex machine!'

Jake roared with laughter. It was too much. Seven threw herself at him.

'Sex machine! Oh, mouse, you sure aren't that and you never will be.' His laughter changed to a grunt of pain as one of her blows found its mark. He caught her wrist with less gentleness than he had intended, stepping back to avoid her wild kicking as he groped for her other flailing hand. 'Not that you aren't sexy in that secretive fashion of yours, but it's a living, breathing, quivering sexuality, not a joyless, mechanical imitation. You, mouse, are the *real thing*.'

The last was said with such fervent wonder that Seven abruptly stopped fighting for anything except the next breath. They stared at each other suspiciously. A strange tingling swept over Seven.

'How did you find me?' She realised he hadn't told her.

'Your sister.'

Seven stiffened incredulously. *'Morgan?'*

She rang your aunt—from Iraq or Iran, I wasn't sure which because the line was so bad—while I was there this afternoon. She was very worried about you. She said you were giving her headaches. She said you were cold and alone and she was afraid for you. Your sister has a very forceful way of expressing herself. She said she knew that it was all my fault that you were pining for love and if anything happened to you she would make damned sure I shared your fate. I told her that was precisely what I wanted.'

'Morgan talked to *you*?' Her sense of betrayal was complete. Only on rare occasions of extreme emotional stress had she and her twin shared thoughts and feelings. And now Jake had violated that part of her, too. 'No!'

He shifted his grip, drew her straining body closer. 'I love you.'

'I hate you,' she said fiercely, wishing that her lie could negate his. 'Leave me alone.'

'Would you have me rip my heart out and lay the bloody thing at your feet?' he whispered roughly into her averted face. 'Because that's what you're asking of me. Your sister's colourful curses aside, I can't abandon you any more than I can abandon Becky——'

'I'm not a child,' she whispered fiercely back, wide eyes holding back the tears. 'I can look after myself——'

'But not as well as I can look after you. I can make you happy. I can be there for you, always . . . when the nightmares come in the night; when you need cool logic to balance the fever in your mind; when you need money or information to save a life or rescue a dream; when you're afraid. I can share all that with you, and more. I can make you laugh. I can make you feel. I can make you safe. I already have a child. What I need to complete my life is you.'

She turned her head to look at him proudly. 'Well, I don't need you.'

'That's not what Morgan said——'

'Morgan said too damned much!'

'I only wish! Actually she didn't say enough. She couldn't pin-point exactly where you were; she said you were north, but not how far. She said you were in a small room, but not where. She said something about a pilgrimage to the past—and I guessed that might mean somewhere near where your parents were killed.'

With a shock Seven realised that Morgan was right. She had been too distraught during her drive to know it, but she had been heading instinctively towards the holiday community further up the coast which had been the scene of the other great upheaval of her life.

'She also said that for some reason she connected you with Anthony Perkins.'

'The actor?' Even Seven found Morgan's cryptic mind difficult to follow sometimes. Jake obviously didn't.

'You mean you didn't notice the name of the motel when you booked in?'

She shook her head. Not consciously, anyway. She hadn't cared if it was a hovel or a Hilton. It was a place to hide.

'The Bates.' He cracked a laugh at her horrified expression. 'The man on the desk told me it was the owner's joke. He isn't even called Bates. But it's good for business, especially since the place is so run-down. It brings in all the thrill-seekers and Hitchcock fans. Not to mention the perverts and weirdos.'

'Like me, you mean.' She had meant it to have a flippancy to match his, but it came out defensively. Jake frowned, then sighed and firmly led her back into the warming lounge.

'We're going to get no peace until we settle this, are we?' He sat her down on the battered couch and joined her closely, so that they were touching from shoulder to knee. 'Doubt that I love you if you like, but are you going to doubt your sister, too? Morgan believed me.'

'Then let her marry you!'

'So at least you believe that much,' he said in satisfaction. 'That I want to marry you.'

'Only because you've suddenly rediscovered father-hood,' said Seven coldly. 'Well, there's no need for noble gestures. I'm not pregnant. I don't need the protection of your name. And I'm not going to give you a baby just to make up for the one you were deprived of!'

He took it without a blink. 'I still want to marry you. You owe me——'

'I owe you *nothing*!' She had been expecting the blow, but not the devastating pain that laid waste her heart. The three little words proved all her worst fears. 'I found your daughter for you, didn't I?' she cried. 'That's what you wanted! I never said that you'd *like* what I found.' She tried to get up, but his arm barred the way. 'There's nothing that I can do to change it now,' she gulped. 'I'm sorry that things turned out the way they did for you, but I couldn't help it—I couldn't know. I'm not omnipotent——'

He let her work herself into a fury of accusation, recognising that she needed the catharsis, knowing it was her way of punishing him for her own doubts. Just so had he used her over the past few weeks. Only when he sensed she was near the end of her wild and tearful tirade did he cut her off, before she had time to regroup her scattered emotions.

'Hush, mouse, I don't blame you for anything. How could I, when you've given me so much more than you've taken? Oh, Seven, for someone who's psychic you're singularly blind to what's right under your neat little nose.' He drew her firmly against his chest and held her there, aware more than ever of her steely fragility, until her sobs faded to hiccups.

'Now. Are you ready to listen?' He tilted up her small face and kissed the sodden violet eyes and pinkened nose. 'First, I want you to close your eyes, and put your head back against my chest, and tell me what you feel.'

Seven opened her mouth to argue, and he kissed it closed, and she blushed to match her nose. She had screeched at him like a fishwife and now he was being tender and teasing and she didn't know what to make of anything any more. So she closed her eyes and allowed him to lean back, pulling her with him, draping herself across his body as she counted the thudding pulse of his heart in his chest.

There was silence except for the crackle of the fire, the steady beat of rain against the iron roof of the cabin, and their soft, slow breathing. Gradually Seven absorbed the knowledge Jake had left someone else to put his precious paper to bed tonight; he had left the daughter he was desperate to know, his ill mother about whom he was still worried, and he had driven a hundred kilometres in the rain on a filthy evening on the flimsy evidence of a psychic reading from a woman he had never met.

'What do you feel?' he murmured softly, nuzzling the burnished top of her head.

'Warm...and...secure,' she admitted, rubbing her face into his shirt.

'Do you know why? That's love. It warms you from the inside out. The more you have of it, the more you want, the more there is... Don't unbutton my shirt, there's a good girl, not until I finish. I've rehearsed this little speech all the way up here and I'm damned if I'm going to be done out of it by a seductive little mouse: the Hastingses told Rebecca I was her father.'

'Oh, Jake——'

'It's all right. She was a bit shocked but——' a crooked grin that didn't quite make the cynical grade '—she likes me. She asked to see me this morning, so that added to my leave-taking panic. She thinks it's neat having two dads, especially since I don't threaten her security in any way.

'She can't consciously recall anything about me, but she feels comfortable with me and that's a start. She doesn't remember much about Sharon Riley, either, thank God. Of course she wanted to know all about the kidnapping. The Hastingses thought she was too young, and maybe she is because she thought it was all pretty cool, but I thought it was better to be honest from the start than make her live through a lot of unpleasant discoveries piecemeal. And I'm thankful to say that Alec and Jessica seem to have got over the worst of their initial paranoia. I went to see them yesterday——' The memory of how he'd felt when he'd come home afterwards to an empty house made his jaw clench. 'I took the draft adoption petition over to the Hastingses to get them to approve it. There's still a lot of red tape to get through, but at least we've laid our intentions out in black and white and initialled them. It felt odd, signing away my daughter when I went through so much for so long to get her back.'

'I'm sorry.' Seven felt a surge of her former guilt.

'I'm not. In a strange way it was a kind of relief. Now, I feel free. I know Becky is happy and that I can be, too. I can be a whole person again, instead of a fragmented one, frantically trying to concrete over the cracks with cynicism. I don't have to be on guard all the time. From the time I met you everything seemed to happen so fast. I, who'd always been in perfect control, was suddenly careering around trying to comprehend the incomprehensible. And I don't mean your psychic abilities, though they were terrifying enough to contend with, I mean the feelings you aroused in me, the fact that I was falling in love with you, that I enjoyed knowing that you were reliant on me for something, even if it was only for physical pleasure.' His voice strengthened with confidence as he spoke.

'When I'm with you I feel as if I have the world at my feet. When I'm inside you, I know I'm home. When you told me you loved me the night before last, it was like the perfect fantasy... so perfect it couldn't be true. I half thought I might have misheard you and I was afraid to ask. I had made so many mistakes in our relationship that I no longer trusted my instincts, which were to jump in and tell you what *I* felt.'

She stirred in his arms. 'How can you love a... a freak?'

'Not a freak. A unique and very, very special person.'

Silence. Not enough? She wanted further proof? With reckless abandon he threw himself to the winds of fortune.

'I know you despise my pseudo-child, the *Clarion*. The truth is—I don't need it any more, it's served its purpose and it takes up too much of my time. There are other things I'd rather do with it now. Besides, I think the Hastingses share your contempt, and feel that a yellow Press baron is not exactly the sort of role-model they really like hanging around Rebecca. You'll make a much more respectable centre to my life, mouse. And there's *our* children—I don't want them to be ashamed of their father. So I'm going to resign as editor and try my hand at writing a novel. I can't guarantee that it won't have a slight tinge of sex and violence. I'm not like my mother, I can't give up my vices.'

'I—I'm not ashamed of what you do. You right a lot of wrongs in your... your...'

'Scurrilous way?' He grinned at her sterling defence. He shrugged, secretly enjoying the soft friction of her breasts against his chest. 'I said I was going to resign, not sell up. I sweated blood over that paper's conception, I can't just walk away and let it be chewed up by some money-hungry conglomerate just because I've had a sudden attack of ethics.' Seven blushed and he chuckled. 'But first things first: I think a long, leisurely honeymoon...don't you? You could take a leave of absence and we could travel...maybe drop in on that sister of yours wherever she might be, and thank her for her cupidity.'

'I haven't said I'll marry you, yet,' she said serenely, savouring the moment.

'You will,' he said, watching the teasing confidence grow in the soft grey eyes. 'You're not the type of woman to be a mistress——'

'Why? What's wrong with me?' She bristled instantly, before the words were even out of his mouth. Didn't he think she was sexy enough?

He laughed. 'I was going to say—"for long". Nothing's wrong with you, that's why I'm in such a hurry to give you my name—not for your protection but for mine. I want every other man in the whole damned world to know that you and I are a fixed alliance. I've told everyone I'm going to marry you. You're going to be hideously embarrassed if it doesn't come off. It'll make headlines in the *Clarion*, and you know how lurid they can be! And now all that's settled——' he pushed her away from him so that he could study her wolfishly '—where's the bed in this joint?'

'You're sitting on it,' giggled Seven. 'The couch folds out. But I'm afraid you...I...we can't——' She took a deep breath. 'You know I told you I wasn't pregnant?' He nodded and she continued stumblingly, bright with embarrassment. 'Well...I only found out yesterday morning...' Disappointment flickered across his face as he realised what she was telling him, and her eyelashes lowered shyly against her flushed cheeks. 'I think that's partly why I ran away,' she whispered. 'I discovered that I was disappointed. Even if there was no shared future for us, I would have loved your baby...'

'I'm sure you will,' he corrected her gently. 'Together we'll play whatever hand fate deals us, mouse. And, since you've admitted that we're as good as married, you don't have to feel sinful when we do *this*...'

'But, Jake——' protested Seven wistfully as he rolled her deftly beneath him.

'I know. No baby tonight. Celibacy is purely a matter of degree, my innocent darling. I've never wanted to pet a mouse before, but there's always a first time for everything. Besides, what better way is there for us to pass a long, cold, winter's night together? I didn't bring a pack of cards... did you?'

To her eternal relief, she hadn't...

EPILOGUE

THE little chubby-cheeked girl screamed, a high-pitched sound of terror that split the peace of the leafy yard.

Her companion bent over her, quickly picking off the plump little arm the spider that had fallen out of the tree.

'It's only a spider, Erin . . . see. It won't hurt you. He's ever so tiny, you could hurt him real easy if you weren't careful.' A thick fall of blonde hair brushed the shimmering nut-brown curls of the toddler as the older girl bent down to show the spider scurrying around her palm.

Erin sniffed, a tear tremblingly readied in the grey-blue eyes as they stared suspiciously at the tiny foe. The boy who had been dangling from the tree above them dropped to the ground and dusted off his hands.

'Let me see.' He nearly toppled Erin in his eagerness to get a look. 'What a cry-baby! I can hardly even see it! I've had spiders ten times the size of that fall on me and I didn't scream.'

'Shut up, Micky, you're scaring Erin,' his sister scolded him. 'She's not even three yet, you know. You were scared of lots of things when you were a baby. Look, Jay, Missy found a spider!'

Jake's hasty steps slowed and Seven, close behind him on the garden path, smiled her relief as her husband inspected his younger daughter's find in Rebecca's outstretched palm.

'Is that what all the noise was about? I thought I heard someone crying,' she said, watching Erin's eyes dry up like magic.

'Erin got a fright but she was pretty brave, for a girl,' offered Micky with a certain protective male contempt. 'She didn't akshully blub, she just yelled real loud.'

'She has a very fine set of lungs, haven't you, wooden top?' Jake knocked lightly on the top of Erin's brown head and she giggled adoringly. 'Why don't you take her up to the house, you two, and see what Mrs Taylor's got for you? She's been baking up a storm all afternoon. I could hardly type for drooling.'

'Yeah?' Rebecca's grin widened at her father's joke, intensifying the likeness between them, and Seven felt the familiar tug of gratitude on her heart-strings. They were so lucky that Rebecca was such a sunny, generous-hearted girl, taking everything in her jaunty stride. She had grown rapidly in the last few months, and was beginning to display a few budding curves as she approached her breathless teens. 'Do you think we could have something to take home tonight, you know, to welcome Mum and Dad back? Mum won't want to bake as soon as she gets back . . .'

'I think Mrs Taylor did murmur something about a spare boysenberry cheesecake,' smiled Jake. Boysenberries were one of Jessica Hastings' weaknesses, although Seven had her doubts that Jessica would be very hungry after the long flight back from Hawaii. She and Alec had spent the last fortnight there on a second honeymoon, and it was symbolic of the trust that existed between the two families that they had felt free to ask Seven and Jake to look after the children in their absence. In truth Seven had been glad of the distraction. She found her boisterous little daughter much more manageable when she had her admired 'big cousins' visiting.

'Don't stuff yourselves too much. I thought that we might stop off at McDonald's on our way to the airport to pick up your parents,' called Jake after the disappearing trio.

'Don't you think Erin's too little to manage a hamburger yet?' scolded Seven lovingly.

'But not for french fries.' Jake grinned.

'You spoil those children...' Seven shook her head as she turned back to the house, waving away a lazy summer bee.

Jake's arms slid around her, just under her breasts, pulling her back against him as he nuzzled the side of her neck. 'It's not spoiling, it's loving. There's a big difference. Mmm...how about we take a little side trip into the bushes?'

'Trip would be right, I'd probably bounce like a ball,' said Seven shakily as her knees weakened. Still, after four years, he could make her tremble with his touch.

'I like you roly-poly.' Jake's hands slid reluctantly away from her ripe breasts to the big mound beneath the loose cotton sun-dress. 'The more of you there is, the more there is to love...' He turned her in his arms, pressing her swollen stomach carefully against his own, sharing her burden, smiling when he felt the healthy kick. 'It amazes me that someone so slender and delicate can carry around such a tough customer. I'm going to have to have a talk with junior, when he finally deigns to make his appearance.'

'Will you mind if it's another girl?' Seven asked happily, certain of his reply, her arms linking around his strong neck.

'As long as both the baby and you are healthy I'll take whatever comes: girl, boy or alien from outer space!'

Seven's expression clouded, her fingers tangling in the hair at the nape of his neck. 'You aren't afraid...you don't wonder whether Erin or the baby might turn out to be...to have...?'

'Your psychic abilities?' Jake's smile was rueful. He had answered the question before and probably would again. 'What should I fear, when I have you as a shining example for a child to follow?' His voice became teasing. 'Why, if it hadn't been for your magical appearance in my life I never would have written my first book, let alone my second, nor that marvellously successful cookbook! I would have still been a "citizen of sleazeville", as I believed you once called me.' He took a growling, mock bite of her ear and there was a long silence as they kissed and the baby kicked playfully between them. Sometimes it was hard to believe that this happy, relaxed, albeit intensely energetic man was the same cynical, aggressive bear of a man she had first fallen in love with.

Seven sighed as he pulled his mouth reluctantly away, her brow pleating dreamily as a thought suddenly occurred. 'I haven't had any spontaneous psychic experiences, for ages, though. I wonder why...'

Jake turned them up the path, one arm across her shoulders, the other hand protectively cupping her belly. 'Did it ever occur to you that maybe your self-imposed isolation and rigid attempts at repression might actually have *intensified* your powers, rather than the reverse? But once you opened yourself up to love you filled up all the dark, lonely places inside yourself. Maybe your psychic ability was connected in some way to a search for a missing part of you, and when you found it you no longer needed the power...'

'The missing part being you, of course,' Seven murmured sweetly, thinking he could well be right. Her disturbing dreams and 'feelings' *had* waned in direct proportion to her growing contentment as a wife and mother, and some-time librarian. Life was very full these days ...

'But of course me,' he said smugly. They took a few more steps in silence and then he said, casually, 'How would you like to come to Paris with me next year, to the Writers' Conference?'

Seven was startled. 'But...the baby. Erin...? How would we manage?' They had gone to the East for their honeymoon and Seven had loved it, but the idea of travelling with two children under five...

'Oh, we'll leave them behind,' said Jake with the same studied casualness. 'The baby will be weaned by then, and it'll only be for three weeks. The odd couple can mind them——' he was referring to the fact that Charlotte and Jane had become extremely close friends, as often as not in each other's houses '—or Becky will con Jessica into a reciprocal offering...'

Seven was stunned, her heart fluttering as wildly as the limbs of her unborn child. 'Leave them...? B-but, Jake, I know how you feel——' He never said anything, but his fear was too deep-rooted to be easily plucked out. He worried whenever Erin was out of sight. Working at home didn't make it any easier. Seven was aware that his frequent coffee breaks were really to check up on her and Erin, to make sure they were safe.

'And it's time I changed how I feel. It's not good for children to grow up feeling they're constantly under surveillance. I don't want to end up as one of those unreasonably possessive fathers who invite rebellion against their authority and embarrass their offspring with their overprotectiveness. I won't say it'll be easy, leaving them, but I'll have you to hold on to...'

'I don't have to go,' said Seven quietly. 'I don't mind staying with the children.' She did. They hadn't been parted, except when Erin was born, since their marriage.

His indigo eyes glowed with dark heat. 'Darling, you don't have to pander to my fears any more. You've been very tolerant with me, spoiled me——'

'That's not spoiling, that's loving——'

'And you deserve some spoiling yourself. The conference is in spring—wouldn't you like to see romantic
Paris with me in the springtime?' His smile promised far
more than mere romance as he mocked the old fear. 'But,
be warned—*you* I have no qualms about keeping under
surveillance. You're just the kind of sweet, feminine,
womanly woman that continental men go mad
over... and not only continentals, come to that...'

Seven laughed, her heart bursting with joy as he swept
her gently around in his arms. They had healed each
other, she and Jake, the shadows of the past at long last
pushed back by the blazing brightness of their love...

Next month's Romances

Each month, you can choose from a world of variety in romance with Mills & Boon. These are the new titles to look out for next month.

NO PLACE TOO FAR Robyn Donald
SECOND TIME LOVING Penny Jordan
IRRESISTIBLE ENEMY Lilian Peake
BROKEN DESTINY Sally Wentworth
PAST SECRETS Joanna Mansell
SEED OF VENGEANCE Elizabeth Power
THE TOUCH OF LOVE Vanessa Grant
AN INCONVENIENT MARRIAGE Diana Hamilton
BY DREAMS BETRAYED Sandra Marton
THAT MIDAS MAN Valerie Parv
DESERT INTERLUDE Mons Daveson
LOVE TAKES OVER Lee Stafford
THE JEWELS OF HELEN Jane Donnelly
PROMISE ME TOMORROW Leigh Michaels

The door to her past awaited – dare she unlock its secrets?

PATRICIA MATTHEWS

MIRRORS

AVAILABLE IN FEBRUARY. PRICE £3.50

Adopted at sixteen, Julie Malone had no memory of her childhood. Now she discovers that her real identity is Suellen Deveraux – heiress to an enormous family fortune.

She stood to inherit millions, but there were too many unanswered questions – why couldn't she remember her life as Suellen? What had happened to make her flee her home?

As the pieces of the puzzle begin to fall into place, the accidents begin. Strange, eerie events, each more terrifying than the last. Someone is watching and waiting. Someone wants Suellen to disappear forever.

WORLDWIDE

A SPECIAL GIFT FOR MOTHER'S DAY

Four new Romances by some of your favourite author
have been selected as a special treat for Mother's Day

A CIVILISED ARRANGEMENT
Catherine George
THE GEMINI BRIDE
Sally Heywood
AN IMPOSSIBLE SITUATION
Margaret Mayo
LIGHTNING'S LADY
Valerie Parv
Four charming love stories for
only £5.80, the perfect gift for
Mother's Day . . . or you can
even treat yourself.

Look out for the special pac
from January 1991.

What did you think of this book?

Spare a few moments to answer the questions on the next page and we will send you a **FREE** Mills & Boon Romance as our thank you.

Mills & Boon we always like to know what you, the readers, think about novels, especially when the stories are a little different - like "No Reprieve" Please can you spare the time to help us now, by filling in this estionnaire and posting it back to us TODAY (No stamp needed).

---

on't forget to fill in your name and address so we know here to send your FREE BOOK.

ease tick the appropriate boxes to indicate your answers. ✔

Did you enjoy NO REPRIEVE by Susan Napier?

| Very much indeed | ❑ | Quite a lot | ❑ |
| Not particularly | ❑ | Not at all | ❑ |

The story carries two themes which you may regard as unusual in a Mills & Boon contempory romance. These are: a) psychic ability and b) child kidnapping. How do you feel about these?

a) psychic ability
It formed an interesting
part of the story ❑

It had no place in
the romance ❑

b) child kidnapping
It formed an interesting
part of the story ❑

It had no place in
the romance ❑

Continued overleaf

3 Did you feel that having both themes in one story was too much, and that you would have preferred one of them only?

Yes ☐   (If so which one? _____)   No

4 When there is a very strong story, the romantic relationship needs to be strong also, to balance this. Did you feel the autho

Achieved this ☐   Did not achieve this ☐

5 If your answer to question 4. was no, which aspect was stron

The romance between the hero and the heroine ☐   The story

6 Do you have any special comment to make about the story, concerning these points or any other.

_____

_____

7 Age group: under 24 ☐   25-34 ☐   35-44 ☐   45-54 ☐   55

8 Have you read more than 6 Mills & Boon romances in the last 2 months?   Yes ☐   No ☐

9 Would you like to read other books of this kind?

Yes ☐   No ☐   Occasionally ☐

10 What is your favourite type of book apart from romantic ficti

_____

Thank you for your help. We hope that you enjoy your FREE boo

Post this page TODAY TO: Mills & Boon Survey, FREEPOST, P.O. Box 236, Croydon CR9 9EL.

Mrs/Ms/Miss/Mr_____   N

Address_____

_____

_____

Postcode _____

You may be mailed with offers from Mills & Boon Ltd. and other respected companies as a result of replying. If you would prefer not to share this opportunity please tick box ☐